The
Slow
Fix

ARSENAL PULP PRESS | VANCOUVER

The Slow Fix

stories

Ivan E. Coyote

ARSENAL PULP PRESS
Suite 200, 341 Water Street
Vancouver, BC
Canada V6B 1B8
arsenalpulp.com

The publisher gratefully acknowledges the support of the Canada Council for the Arts and the British Columbia Arts Council for its publishing program, and the Government of Canada (through the Book Publishing Industry Development Program) and the Government of British Columbia (through the Book Publishing Tax Credit Program) for its publishing activities.

This is a work of fiction. Any resemblance of characters to persons either living or deceased is purely coincidental.

Earlier versions of these stories appeared in *Xtra! West*

Text and cover design by Shyla Seller
Cover photograph by Dan Bushnell
Photograph of Ivan E. Coyote by Laura Sawchuk

Printed and bound in Canada on 100% post-consumer recycled paper

Library and Archives Canada Cataloguing in Publication:

Coyote, Ivan E. (Ivan Elizabeth), 1969-
    The slow fix / Ivan E. Coyote.

ISBN 978-1-55152-247-0

    I. Title.

PS8555.O99S56 2008   C813'.6   C2008-904099-6

This book is dedicated to my grandmothers, Florence Daws and Patricia Cumming, for their strength and spirit. They just don't make them like they used to.

CONTENTS

By Any Other Name

I learned most of what I know about being a man from my Uncle Rob. Uncle Rob has never let the fact that I was declared female at birth get in the way of our male bonding, and I've always loved him best for it.

Uncle Rob taught me how to fish, drive a standard, light a match off of my front tooth, and open a beer with a Bic lighter. He taught me how to make a fist, turn into a skid, light a fire, and shoot a gun. He passed on to me everything he has ever managed to learn about women, and all the Zippo tricks he has ever been shown. He taught me how to tell a story, and how to hold my liquor. All the important stuff. Some of the family reckon I look more like my Uncle Rob than I do my own father, and everyone agrees I look just like my Dad.

Uncle Rob and Aunt Cathy flew to Vancouver last week, because Rob had an appointment with a fancy eye doctor. Whitehorse General Hospital is equipped to handle your basic medical tests and common ailments, but anything involving a specialist or an expensive machine requires a trip to the big city. Rob called me from the hotel and told me to round up the stray cousins and bring the girlfriend; he was taking us all out for dinner. Cousin Darryl's brand new baby had somehow turned into a seven-year-old girl, and I hadn't seen my cousin Garth since Grandma Pat came to town for her knee replacement three years ago.

I rarely bring a date along to family functions, because

more than two or three of us in one room can be hazardous, especially if you are shy, offend easily, clean and sober, or don't eat meat. The way my family demonstrates our love and affection for each other has occasionally been mistaken for verbal abuse by outsiders, so I usually don't take the risk.

But I knew she could hold her own; she is smart and strong and can take a joke. She loves fishing and hates hippies. There was common ground, and she might just fit right in. Besides, I figured, how could she love me and not like my Uncle Rob? He was the man who taught me everything I knew, and I look just like him.

The appetizers arrived in the middle of a raucous debate about flatulence and love: was unabashed farting in front of the fairer sex an expression of intimacy, or the sign of the death of romance? Was pulling the covers over her head actually a form of foreplay? Was our whole family actually lactose intolerant, or did we just not chew our food enough?

My sweetheart was unfazed, and retained her appetite. Maybe she really was the perfect girl for me.

By the time our entrees arrived, the talk had turned to embarrassing stories from when I was a kid, how I had panic attacks when forced into a dress for weddings, and how I finally gave in and wore a satin gown with dyed-to-match pumps to my high school graduation, just like the normal girls did.

"She looked so pretty," said Aunt Cathy solemnly, like she was giving my eulogy.

"I looked like a drag queen."

Darryl shook his head. "I can't imagine cousin Ivan in a dress."

"I can't imagine calling her Ivan." Cathy stabbed a bit of broccoli with her fork. "She'll never be Ivan to me. That's just, like, your writing name, right? Nobody actually calls you Ivan in person, do they?"

Cathy asks me this, even though the entire table had been calling me Ivan all night. I stopped using my birth name over a decade ago, but Cathy likes to pretend she doesn't know this because it makes her uncomfortable. I love her enough to allow her this tiny corner of cozy denial, and my continued silence on the matter helps to hold up my half of her little charade.

I have lots of people who call me Ivan. I only have the one Aunt Cathy. She has never understood why I changed my name, or why I vote NDP. I've never understood why she collects Santa Claus dolls, or how she can smoke menthols. It doesn't mean we love each other any the less for it.

"I've always called Ivan Ivan," states cousin Darryl, God bless him. No wonder everyone thinks he's gay.

"Are we allowed to have dessert?" squeaks second cousin Rachael.

"Anybody want to try a prawn? Going, going, gone." Rob speaks around a mouthful of his dinner.

"Don't chew and talk at the same time, Robert. You'll set a bad example. There are children present." Cathy half-feigns disgust and backhands her husband in the upper arm, right where his shirtsleeve stopped and his tanline

11

started. This signaled the official change of subject.

"Set a bad example for little Rachael?" Rob smirks, rubbing his arm where she had whacked him one. "It's already too late for Rachael, too late for all of them. I saw it on the Learning Channel. A child's personality is fully formed by the time they turn three. We might as well relax and let it all hang loose. The kid is already who she's gonna be, all we can do now is love her. It's out of our hands. "

Rob leans across the table to pinch one of my fries. "Did Garth tell you him and Allison are getting hitched in Fiji? Cath and I are going. You and your lovely lady friend should come too. I'll rent us a boat and we can go fishing. The wedding is still over a year away, so start saving up. Maybe even Darryl will have a girlfriend by then, and we'll all go. A family that fishes together stays together, isn't that what they say? And you two girls would love Fiji. It's the perfect place for you, really: it's beautiful there, and the policemen wear skirts."

Welcome Wagon

When I got back from my last stretch of road-gigs there was a message blinking on my brand new landline. This was unusual—I'm on the road so much that my friends have my cellphone number programmed into their speed dials, and the only person I had given the new number to was my grandmother, and she doesn't believe in leaving messages.

The voice belonged to a stranger. "Hullo. My name is Pauline, and I'm calling on behalf of the Welcome Wagon. We heard you are new to Squamish, so if you would like us to drop by for a visit, call me back and let me know."

I called her back immediately. Of course I would love a visit from the Welcome Wagon. It was just this kind of small-town hospitality that I had left the big city for, I told her, and sure, Friday morning at ten would be perfect.

I spent most of Thursday scouring my house. I mopped, washed the windows, and coerced my girlfriend into baking a fruit crumble. She seemed to think I was overdoing things a bit.

"Isn't it supposed to be the other way around? I thought the Welcome Wagon was supposed to bake *you* a fruit crumble. I thought that was the whole point."

"We'll pop it back into the oven just before she gets here, so the house smells like baking, like I cook in here all the time."

She shook her head at me, and I resumed hand scrubbing the grout between the tiles on the kitchen floor.

By nine a.m. on Friday, my mood had shifted. I woke up worrying that the Welcome Wagon lady was rich and lived in a spotless mansion at the top of the mountain. I woke up thinking she would notice that my apartment building needed a paint job and that the hallways smelled like someone else's supper. I woke up embarrassed that I had hardly any furniture yet, and only owned two towels.

By nine-thirty I was convinced that the Welcome Wagon's job wasn't to welcome people at all, it was actually a covert tool of social control, an organized posse of judgmental socialites sent in to survey the homes of newcomers. Pauline was going to show up, look around, drop off some muffins, and then report back to head office that a self-employed homosexual artist had somehow infiltrated the town's perimeter, and that my dishcloth didn't even match my tea towels. How could I have fallen for a transparent scam like this?

Pauline turned out to be a soft-spoken slender woman with the remnants of an English accent. She was on a diet and turned down a piece of fruit crumble. She took her coffee black and got right down to business. And business it really was.

Her basket wasn't full of muffins, like I'd imagined it. It was full of gift certificates and small gifts from various businesses in town. I was welcomed to Squamish with a bag of cat-treats, a bottle of Vitamin C, a funeral parlour pen, and an Extra Value meal from McDonald's. I had to sign a form saying I had received the aforementioned merchandise from Pauline on behalf of the Welcome Wagon, to ensure that Pauline had indeed welcomed me properly and not shirked her duties and just kept all the key chains and cat treats for herself.

"So how long have you lived in Squamish?" I asked her, once all the paperwork had been filled out.

"Just since June." Pauline had a way of exhaling when she talked, which made it sound like everything she said was accompanied by a little sigh.

I raised my eyebrows. "And you're already working for the Welcome Wagon?" I guess I had been expecting a more long-term resident.

"I resurrected it myself after we had been here for three months, and none of the neighbours had come around yet to introduce themselves. I was out of my mind with loneliness, and I thought it would be a good way to meet people."

I sat up straight. "So you don't find this place all that friendly either, huh?" I found this oddly comforting, to know it wasn't just me.

Pauline stared down into her coffee, trying to hide the tears that threatened to spill over her bottom lashes. "I've almost stopped crying whenever my friends from home ring me up. It's not like this in Nova Scotia. People there know how to be neighbours."

We chatted a bit more, and when Pauline left she pressed her phone number into my hand, saying maybe we could go hiking together sometime.

"What does it mean when the Welcome Wagon lady is crying from the lack of new friends?" I asked my sweetheart. She agreed that it wasn't a good sign, and served me up some warm fruit crumble.

The next day we packed up and headed south into Vancouver, a ninety-minute ride. "Notice how the air smells all smoggy?" I commented as we crossed the bridge. "Listen to how loud it is here. All the traffic, and the sirens. There is never anywhere to park. It's not like this in Squamish."

I spent the day in my old neighbourhood, on the Drive, picking up my mail, doing some banking, drinking too much coffee, running into people I knew, people who were glad to see me. Wendy from the credit union smiled wide as she stamped the backs of my cheques. I almost leaned across the counter and kissed her, it was so nice to be known, so great to not be asked to see some identification.

"So how are things in Squamish?" she asked me.

"Great, great. It's really beautiful, and quiet. It's so quiet out there." I said, like a mantra. I had said the same thing to everyone who had asked me that question, over and over, all day.

I'm hoping that if I repeat it enough, I'll eventually start believing it myself.

Open Sesame

I'm starting to get used to the sound of my new life in Squamish. Every place has its own sound; its own flavour of normal noises. Part of making this new place home for me is teaching my ears what familiar should sound like. There are big trucks with engine brakes that growl around the corners on the highway. There are country-and-western-slash-classic-rock-inspired parties in the building next door, and thus whooping noises and hollering are somewhat commonplace, and for the most part are to be ignored. A siren, once an auditory backdrop in my place on Victoria Drive, will now bring me along with the rest of my neighbours out onto our balconies, coffee cups in hand, just to see what all the excitement is about.

Everything sounds different here, but mostly it's the sound of kids playing. I'm not talking about the fevered cadence of a fifteen-minute recess across the street. Kids can still really play outside in Squamish. I'm talking about the sun-ripened drawl of kids with a whole summer stretched out in front of them, and nothing to do but ride bikes in the courtyard or catch bugs in jam jars.

Squamish is the outdoor recreation capital of Canada, or so the sign on the highway proclaims, but not if your parents can't afford rock climbing gear or kite-surfing lessons. One rainy day I listened to six kids amuse themselves all afternoon by tumbling Matchbox cars and Barbies down the stairwell, and opening and closing the door for anyone who came in or left the building. My little dog could have ten walks a day if I said yes every time one of the little girls knock on my door to ask if Goliath can come out to play.

The kids build bike ramps out of rocks dragged up from the river and worn-out bits of plywood, and then ride around in endless aimless circles popping wheelies and taking jumps until the lady who heads up the strata council dismantles them one night after bedtime, and then the cycle begins again.

I'm starting to learn their names now, who is who's little brother, and which building they live in. So far, Kristy and Mouse are my favourites. Kristy is the oldest I think, with her T-shirt stretched over her plump middle and her arms often crossed to hide her tiny boobies. Kristy watches everything all the time, and doesn't miss a thing that goes on anywhere. She is definitely the one to ask if you want the goods on anyone. Then there is Mouse, her other half.

How can you tell a tomboy before she even opens her mouth, from inside the car with the windows rolled up? It is something about the way she stands, how her jeans hang below her hips and the cuffs are long enough that she wears holes in them with the heels of her Bay sneakers.

Maybe it takes one to know one.

Mouse watched me pack stuff out of my car into my apartment one day.

"That a microphone stand?" she asked me out of the corner of her mouth.

"Sure is," I told her.

Mouse squinted into the sun. "You gotta microphone to go with it?"

"Sure do."

"Maybe can I borrow it one day? I'm extremely responsible, ask anyone."

I scratched my chin, pretending to think about it. "Let's see...should I lend the amplification equipment out to the children?"

Silence hung between us. Mouse opened her eyes really wide, hanging there for an answer.

"Sure, I can do that." I tell her, and a smile explodes across her face. "But I have to meet your mom first, and ask her if it's okay with her, too."

Mouse nods like a hammer drill. My heart warms, and then remembers to go cold at the reality of it all.

This is my big fear, you see. I'm pretty sure I'm the only queer residing in the Westway Village apartments, and for some reason I pass as a young man a lot more here, at least with the grown-ups. Children, in my experience, are far less likely to be fooled by shallow gender stereotypes than their parents are; kids hardly ever mistake me for a boy or a man, or maybe they just care a lot less what gender I am.

They're more interested in whether or not I will lend them my microphone or play street hockey with them.

What I worry about is that the kids will go home and tell their mom the nice lady named Ivan lent them the microphone, and the mom will freak out about a homosexual interacting with the children. Some folks have a thing about queers being around their kids. Even though the statistics show that it is far more likely that their new boyfriend or their husband or their brother will be the one molesting their son or daughter, still they worry more about the homosexual up the street.

I never understood this, but it is the way things are. The only homo on the block has to be careful when befriending the kids. Which is kinda sad, when you consider how much some of these kids could use a friend.

"Let me have a chance to meet your mom first, Mouse, and we'll see."

All day yesterday the kids were busy furiously constructing a fort in the bushes alongside the little river behind my building. When I loaded my bags and the dogs into the car to head into the city, they popped their heads out of the blackberry bushes to inform me that if I could guess the password, they would open the trap door and show me their fort.

"Open sesame?" I guessed, feeling old and kind of uncool even as the words left my mouth.

"Ppfhhh." The nine-year-old who is the older brother of Brendan snorted and scoffed at me. "Open sesame. How gay. It's Yo Mama, dumbhead."

Kristy stood up for me first. "Don't call her that. She's cool. She lives in my building."

Schooled

Yesterday I spent the day in a high school in Burnaby, telling stories to the grade tens. I was surprised how nervous I was. I tell stories all over the place, often to people who in real life are much more intimidating than a couple hundred fifteen-year-old strangers should be, but right from the time the alarm went off it was there, the big ball of nervous. It hung there in my gut, between my ribs and my belly, all waxy and electric.

The face in the mirror looked pale and rumpled. "That's just perfect," I told my reflection. "A zit. Right in the middle of your chin. On the first day of school."

It's something about the hallways that does it to me, the way sounds are amplified by the polished tiles and painted lockers, all sharp edges and canned echoes. Just the sound of a high school makes me fifteen again.

It didn't help much that all five of us poets and storytellers had to wait in the office for the English teacher to come and escort us to the auditorium. Lined up with our asses slouched in the plastic chairs outside the principal's office, in between the photocopier and the water cooler, the rest of them joked and told anecdotes. I was the quiet one for once, trying to breathe around the inflatable lump in my throat and wondering why my toes were sweating so profusely.

The teacher that had organized the reading was cool; the kind of teacher who would think that poetry in high school was a good thing. Her classroom was the one with the beaded curtain, and the kids who were wrestling or kicking each other in the ass in the hallways didn't straighten up or act like pretend angels when she came around the corner. She explained to us over her shoulder as we walked that the crowd for the lunch-hour show might be a little smaller than they had expected, because today the student council was auctioning off elves in the gymnasium, plus a representative from the community college was answering questions and handing out pamphlets outside the library. We had competition, she told us, but assured us we would have a good house for the afternoon sessions, when attendance was mandatory.

She took us into a place she called the dance room, which meant it looked like a small gym with mirrors lining the walls. She apologized for the fact that we were required to remove our shoes, because they marked up the floor. For some reason this made me uncomfortable. I was about to tell queer stories to a bunch of teenagers, and I wanted my shoes. My sock feet left little sweaty tracks behind if I stood in one place for too long. Two of the other poets were wearing odd socks, and this made me blush. We were here to prove that being a spoken word performer was a viable career option, and I felt that not owning a pair of socks that matched might undermine our position. Then I reminded myself that they had both just come off of a long tour, and I should be glad they were wearing any socks at all. The kids all had to take their shoes off too, which they did in an orderly fashion as they filed into the room. Quite a few of them had on odd socks as well. I changed my position on the matter immediately, thinking maybe it would be something we could bond with them over. Odd socks didn't mean you were poor. Odd socks meant you were a non-conformist.

It turned out that the kids were great. They listened and laughed in all the right places, and asked really smart questions. One kid asked us what the meaning of life was, saying that he had read somewhere that if you asked enough people, one of them might just have an answer. Then he asked me what my favourite Led Zeppelin album was. I told him *Led Zeppelin IV*, and he nodded, like I had passed his invisible test.

Somewhere between classes I relaxed a bit and started to have fun. Sure, there was a couple of kids slouched along one side of the classroom at the back of the room who already could grow sideburns and snickered and rolled their eyes the whole time, but for the most part they were interested, and engaged. I kept telling myself that I wasn't there to change the mind of the beefy guy in the back with the almost full goatee. I was there for the kid I couldn't see yet, the kid who was seeing me for the first time. The kid who walked the edges of the hallways, one hand trailing the lockers and the walls, hoping they won't be waiting for him at the bus stop today. The kid who hides his *Muscle and Fitness* magazines behind a ceiling tile in his closet, when his brothers can read them openly because they are not like him. For the girl who doesn't know yet but her parents do. That was who I was there for.

The cool teacher escorted us through the woodworking shop in between classes to a patchy corner of lawn you couldn't see from any windows in the school, so we could have a smoke. The shop was almost empty, because the bell hadn't rung yet. There was a skinny boy with glasses screwing two bits of wood together with a cordless drill. He nodded at the cool teacher as we shuffled past.

"Hello Vanessa," the cool teacher nodded back at the kid, and I did a double take. The teacher winked at me, and I smiled. All day, I had been searching for signs that things were different than they were when I was in school, that things were getting easier for queer kids, that we really had come a long way, baby. I had overlooked the most obvious sign. Of course things were changing. I was here, wasn't I?

Home Sweat Home

Not one of my friends even feigned surprise when I announced I was moving back to Vancouver. Turns out they had a pool going: the piano player reckoned I would last until February, whereas the hockey player had her money on November. Some figured I would want to come back by Christmas, but pride and belligerence would force me to hold out until spring. When I found out my friends were placing bets on my return, I was tempted to stick it out, just to save a little face, but soon came to my senses. Having to be right was a terrible reason not to correct the wrong that was me living in Squamish. Maybe I *had* matured.

What was the final straw? Was it when the leaves all fell, revealing a summer's worth of McDonald's detritus strewn in a soggy donut around the park where I walked the dogs? Was it when the cute rock-climber girls all went back to school and the rednecks didn't? Was it the gang of teenage boys that followed me home from the store that night, swilling something stolen from the parents' liquor cabinet out of a two-litre Coke bottle, too close and too loud to be just being friendly?

It was two Friday nights ago, when the guy who lives right below me, whom I affectionately call the Missing Link, stopped me in the hall on my way up from the laundry room. He had a three-quarters-empty case of beer under one arm and was only looking out of one eye at a time, rattling his key ring around in one hand in the hopes of finding one that would work in his front door.

"Dude," he said, "I gotta tell you, man, I thought you were a fucking faggot until I met your girlfriend. She's hot."

"Thank you," I said, mostly because I wasn't quite sure how to respond to a comment like that, and I was pretty sure he thought he was complimenting me. Anything else would have been, well, un-neighbourly, not to mention dangerous. I no longer risk angering men whose biceps are bigger around than my thighs.

I locked my door behind me and leaned up against it. There was no more pretending. I wanted to go home. I missed East Vancouver. Not only was I growing tired of looking over my shoulder, my wardrobe habits were already starting to slide. It was starting to be okay to go to the video store with my boots untied. I knew what happened next, the evidence was all around me. I had to get out of Squamish before track pants became acceptable evening wear, or I got gay-bashed. I knew both were just a matter of time.

Me and my sweetheart began the process of searching for dog-friendly housing in Vancouver again. She had just been given the word that her landlord planned to renovate the entire house in April, and they were all going to have to move.

It seemed impossible, but the rents had gone up even in the five months I had been living in Squamish. It appears the yuppies have been buying up character houses in my beloved neighbourhood faster than you can say half a million dollars, renovating the basement, renaming it a garden suite, and getting the tenants to pay the better part of their mortgage payment for them. Some call this a good investment. I call it a crime. Wait until the yuppies find out that the artists and working people are being priced out of East Vancouver, and that all that "character" they moved to our neighbourhood for has had to relocate, in search of affordable housing. One day they will wake up and head to the coffee shop, to find only investment bankers and corporate lawyers to talk to. We gave them Kitsilano after the seventies were over, and just look what they did with it. Who will they rent out their garden suites to when that happens? All that beige paint and laminate flooring will have been for nothing.

Last year, after my house burned down – which prompted my move to Squamish – the last thing I wanted was another absentee landlord who didn't care about his house. Now all I wanted was an absentee landlord who didn't care about his house. A home where I was allowed to have dogs, cook meat, paint colours on the walls, and be a writer.

It wasn't on craigslist, and it wasn't in the papers. We found it the old-fashioned way, walking up and down the streets we liked and looking for For Rent signs. It didn't look like much from the outside, and the inside wasn't much better, at least at first glance. We had to squint, and imagine what a little paint could do, and how there were probably wood floors underneath the tattered carpet. Two bedrooms, the whole attic, and a sunroom off the back where I could write. I liked the landlord right off the bat; how he shrugged about the dogs and told my girlfriend how good-looking she was, like a movie star. How he winked at me, how one of the lenses of his glasses had fallen out and he had glued it back in with what looked like tub and tile caulking.

He showed us pictures of his kids, and bragged about how they all went to university, and gave us a card to get twenty-five percent off of dental work at his son's practice in the West End. We filled out a lease that read NO DRUNK-ARDS PLEASE across the top, and then he insisted we drink some of his neighbour's U-brew wine with him. He wouldn't stop talking, and I couldn't stop smiling.

"You girls can fix it up nice, just like the two ladies on the main floor did. You will like them, same lifestyle as you." He winked again. "I don't bother you, you don't bother me, I don't raise the rent, and we are all lucky."

The Curse?

I called my cousin up the other day, and partway through our usual gab he informed me that Layla, his stepdaughter, had some very exciting news.

"Can I tell Ivan, or do you want to tell her yourself?" he asked her from his end of the living room couch.

I heard her almost teenage voice in the background, saying it was fine; he could go ahead and tell me.

"Layla got her period this morning." He sounded proud, like she had won the science fair, or got straight As, something along those lines.

I was unsure how I should respond, but they both sounded happy on their end of the phone, so I asked to speak to Layla directly.

"Congratulations," I told her. "It sounds like some sort of a celebration is in order. You have anything in mind?"

I couldn't help but think back to my big day. My mom was out of town at the time, and when I called my Dad upstairs to ask him what I should do, he panicked on the other side of the bathroom door, emptied out my mom's drawer in the other bathroom, whacked his toe on a doorjamb, swore profusely, and then tossed me a box of anal suppositories, mistaking them, I believe, for some sort of feminine hygiene product. Neither of us were proud of me, and we never mentioned the subject again.

"Can you take me to see *The Corpse Bride*?" Layla asked me. "And can we have popcorn?"

"That is an excellent plan," I told her. "I'll pick you up at 6:30. It's a date."

On my way over, I pondered whether or not I should discuss the merits of menstruation with my young friend. It was obvious that this was a brave new world, and that Layla was being brought up to believe that her period was not a dirty female secret like it was when I was twelve years old, and this was a good thing. But I wondered if it would be strange for her to chat about it all with her butch relatives, or if my silence on the matter would be noted.

"So, you got your period, huh?" I asked her as she did up her seatbelt.

She nodded casually.

"Cool," I said, feeling like a gigantic dork. "Way to go."

And that was the end of that.

A couple of days later, I got mine. I plodded through the slush on the sidewalks to the corner store for a box of tampons. I went up both aisles twice, and couldn't find them.

Finally the guy behind the counter asked me if I needed any help finding something.

Normally, I would just shake my head and grab a can of soup, so I didn't have to say the word tampon to the guy behind the counter at the corner store, but this was a brave new world. I needed to get with the times, and cast off my shame and embarrassment, for the sake of young girls everywhere.

"Uh, yeah, I'm looking for tampons," I said.

"For what?" There were two other guys waiting to buy their cigarettes, and they both looked at me.

"Tampons."

He shook his head again, and cupped one hand around his ear, signaling that he couldn't hear me, I needed to speak up. I considered my options. I could scream out in a crowded corner store that I needed a box of tampons, or I could run for the door.

I chose the door.

The next corner store had an ample supply, and I let out a huge breath I hadn't realized I had been holding in. I took the box up to the counter along with a couple of other items I didn't really need, for cover.

I don't know why I am uncomfortable saying the word tampon out loud, or acknowledging the fact that I, like almost all estrogen-based organisms my age, get my period. Maybe it is residual Catholicism; maybe it is because most corner store guys think I am a young man on a supply run for his girlfriend or mother. Or maybe I just don't like to talk tampons with strangers.

"What brand is the best?" The guy behind this counter held up my tampons for the entire world to take notice of.

"I beg your pardon?" I was hoping I hadn't heard him properly, that this was not happening to me.

"There are so many brands to choose from, and different sizes, too. I never know what I should order, so I ask my lady customers, which one is the best?"

There was another guy behind me in line now, holding a box of Kraft dinner and a loaf of white bread. He raised an eyebrow.

I felt a sudden rivulet of sweat in my armpits. Running for yet another door at this juncture would send the message that tampons are, indeed, a shameful topic. This thoughtful merchant had come to me for help in serving the needs of women throughout the entire neighbourhood, and it would behoove me to behave accordingly.

I took a deep breath and spoke in a calm, confident tone. "Well, I would say that it is definitely a matter of personal choice, similar to choosing the right condom for the job. A variety of sizes would obviously be a good thing, as there are many sizes of ... vaginas out there."

He nodded and leaned forward, interested.

"And as for brand, I always prefer the ones without an applicator for, you know, environmental reasons, but again, I can only speak for my own ... I can only speak for myself. I guess as wide a variety as you can carry would be my answer."

He thanked me and rang in my purchases. "Will you be needing a bag today?"

I nodded, and stuffed my tampons in, out of sight for the walk home. "You gonna watch the hockey game tonight?"

He shook his head. "I don't follow the hockey. Myself, I like cricket."

I shrugged. The guy behind me shook his head and stepped up to the counter as I headed for the door.

"Cricket, hey?" He was still shaking his head. "Well, each to their own."

To Whom It May Concern:

I don't want to sound like someone's grandmother or anything here, but really, would it be so hard to pick up a phone and call? You don't even have to call me, just call anyone, your brother, your dad, any of us, just to let us know that you are alive. We all talk, you see, hoping that one of us has seen you, or heard word, or even heard a rumour.

I'm not even the worrying kind, you know me, I get really busy too and forget to keep in touch and miss my cousin's birthday or whatever, just like everyone else, and I'm definitely not usually the type to get on anyone's case for stuff like this. It's just that the last time I saw you, you had lost about thirty-five pounds and the crystal meth was starting to turn your back teeth black, and the newspapers and the streets are full of stories about irreversible brain damage and psych wards brimming with lost souls stricken by this addiction, and, well, I worry. It's not like you're backpacking in Europe and just forgot to send a postcard. I don't care about broken promises or the money you owe anyone. I do care that your brother and your dad spent another Christmas wondering where you were, and that they are running out of reasons you haven't seen your niece and nephew. I can't help but care about that, but even that I would let slide.

Some guy asked me for change outside of the bank today. He looked skinny and drawn and nervous, just like you did the last time I ran into you on the Drive, and for some unexplainable reason I felt like punching him. Instead I took a deep breath and asked him when was the last time he called his mother?

The self-help books and the twelve-step doctrines would probably feed me some line right now about how no one can really help you until you are ready to help yourself and to not to allow myself to feel hurt that I haven't heard from you in almost a year, that it is your addiction governing your behaviour right now and not you. But I call bullshit on that. We have known each other since we were kids, I would and have done anything to help you, and I deserve better than this.

This not knowing. Remember when I dragged you off the street and let you sleep it off for days and fed you and helped you track down the bits and pieces of your life so you could start putting them back together? Back then you said you were done with it all, you were ready, you wanted to change your life, and you needed my help.

I told you that night on the back porch I would do what-ever it took, anything in my power to see you through this time, but that I had one condition. My one condition wasn't even that you stay clean, because I know what a demon the meth is, and I didn't want you tossing me out with the clean and sober bathwater if you backslid. My one condition was that you didn't lie to me anymore, that if you used I wanted to hear about it from you. No more bullshit.

Maybe that is why you haven't called, maybe the truth was something you thought I wouldn't want to hear, or something you weren't prepared to say out loud.

I asked after you at your favourite old coffee shop the other day. The owner's grandson, the cute one, he surprised me by saying yes, he had seen you, and that you were looking great, that you had cleaned up and were living in the suburbs somewhere, and working construction.

I let out the long breath with your name on it that I had been holding for almost a year, and went straight home to call your brother. I was so glad to have word that you were alive and well that it took me a couple of days to get around to wondering why you hadn't gotten in touch with anyone.

The guy who first said 'No news is good news' obviously never had a best friend fighting the ice.

And the guy who coined the phrase "fair-weather friend" never met either of us. I once told you I knew that if ever I found myself in your shoes, I had every faith you would be there for me, and you hugged me in place of a yes.

I think of you whenever I swim in a lake, whenever I pass a rusty pick-up truck on the highway, whenever I see the northern lights or a blue-eyed dog. I miss you whenever I hit my thumb with a hammer, ride my bike, or walk past a lawn that needs mowing.

I'm not writing this to judge you, or to make you feel guilty. I'm writing this to let you know that whenever you are ready, I will be here. I refuse to give up on you. The fire that burned my house down spared the garage, so I still have most of the tools you stored at my place. A couple of times I had to laugh out loud at the same time as I was cursing your name, as I've moved around a lot since my house burned down, and I must really fucking love you, because I can't think of anyone else I would move an entire set of free weights five times for, myself included.

I will pick up that phone whether you are still using or not, and I will listen to you whether your news is rosy or rainy. I want you to know that I meant what I said on the back porch that night, no matter what. No bullshit. A lot of things have changed for both of us since then, but not my home phone number.

Oh yeah, and my grandmother says to say hello.

The Slow Fix

I've never been the sort to fix what ain't broke. If something works for me, or almost works for me, or pretty much works for me the better part of the time, chances are I'm going to leave it be. I still have the same savings account my Uncle John opened for me the summer I turned nine, and I've never spent my last ten dollars because it was my first ten dollars. I drive my laundry twenty-two blocks because I like the way the lady there smiles at me the same way she did when I first asked her for change back in 1991, when I lived on East Georgia. I've had the same barber, the guy at the corner of Charles and Commercial, since 1989. Back then he charged ten bucks for a haircut, and seventeen years later it has gone up to a whopping $13.50.

When Daniel first started cutting my hair, he was single and flat-tummied, and so was I. He would neatly fold and tuck a paper towel under and over the collar of the plastic poncho thing they Velcro around your neck, so no little stray hairs would make me itch later.

"Same same, like always?" Daniel has asked me this once a month for almost two decades.

This is where I nod, and say, "Not too short, or you'll make me look like a dyke."

Then we always smile, as if I could easily blend into heterosexual anonymity, if only he is careful not to take too much off of my bangs.

Back in the day, Daniel would go on about how he was

never going to have kids, how they were too expensive, and then he would point at the red sports car parked outside his side window, and wink at me.

Now his kids are twelve and ten, and him and the woman who used to rent the chair next to him commute to work together in the same minivan, and he doesn't wink as much, not with the wife around.

Last summer Daniel opened a second shop on Robson Street. He told me that as of next month, I would have to go downtown if I still wanted him to cut my hair, and that his wife and new employee were going to stay behind and run the old place. I didn't tell him that I wouldn't go to Robson Street with a gun to my head, not for any reason, even a thirteen-dollar haircut. It was just not my way. I don't get my hair cut on Robson Street; I get my hair cut at the corner of Charles and Commercial. I didn't tell him that I was broken-hearted at his nonchalant disregard for our relationship, at how he could just turn his back on seventeen years of satisfactory haircuts with a casual wave of his scissor hand. I thought about finding a new barber altogether, but that just seemed like too much change all at once.

I ended up getting his new employee to cut my hair the next month, which was weird because the only instructions I had ever given Daniel were "same, same, like always," which didn't work much for the new girl. She even tried to bust out a blow dryer on me, which was terrifying in its wrongness.

The second or third time the new girl cut my hair, Daniel's wife was putting the final touches on the neckline of a beefy guy in his early twenties in the chair next to me. He was going on about this fucking faggot who cut his hair the last time, and how the fag wouldn't cut the back in a straight line how he liked it, but instead the homo tried to talk him into a more natural neckline and how he was forced to tell the fucking pansy that he didn't want his faggoty advice and that in fact he didn't even want him touching him with his AIDS-ridden fairy hands anyways...

And so on, like that. I tried to tell myself to just keep my mouth shut and get my hair cut, that it was sunny out and up until that point I had been having a great day, and that I had a gig that night and I needed to conserve my energy....

And so on, like that. But then I looked up and saw the two dykes waiting in the chairs by the door, and I thought of how I had been coming here for haircuts since this mouthy fucker was in training pants, and that this was my neighbourhood, and there were only six of us in the room, and I knew for sure that three of us were queer, and yet five of us were remaining silent while one of us was spewing hate unabated, and I turned to the guy and told him to shut his ignorant mouth.

He stopped talking for a minute, and his ignorant mouth hung open. I told him that he was talking about my family, and that I would never come into his neighbourhood and sit next to him and talk about his family like that, and then he said a bunch more ignorant things that were neither witty nor interesting enough to repeat here, and besides, we've heard them all before anyway, and then he tossed a twenty on the counter and left.

Leaving me, the two other dykes, and the two hair-dressers draped in an uncomfortable coat of quiet. To break the silence, I started chatting up the new girl about North Korea, where she had lived up until two years ago. She told me things were different there; for instance, if I had done what I had just done in North Korea, I could have been arrested. I forgot to ask her if she meant I could have been arrested just for being queer, or for refusing to take abuse for being queer.

Last week I noticed that the windows of Daniel's shop were covered in newspaper, and a sign in the front announced that a clothing store was opening soon. I knew right away that I would never set foot in the new hipster clothing store just on principle, and that I needed to find a new barber. Just as well, I thought, because ever since Daniel left, things have never been the same same, like always.

It Works Like This

I have to admit, I thought saying goodbye to my bachelor-hood was going to hurt a lot more than it actually did. After living on my own for thirteen years, the concept of a room-mate seemed uncivilized somehow, and the thought of living with my lover used to make my necktie feel too tight.

I had grown attached to working in my underwear and eating soup straight out of the pot. Perpetrating these and some of my more unmentionable habits on a partner seemed somehow ungentlemanly, and changing things about myself that I personally didn't have a problem with seemed highly unlikely.

We moved in together last December, and aside from an ongoing struggle for domestic dominance between me and her cat, it has been bliss. There have been some adjustments, for sure, but nothing that left me longing for the good old days. Mostly, I'd say it has just been educational.

For instance, one might think that jumping into the shower while she is blow-drying her hair is acceptable behaviour, but it turns out that I had much to learn about the physical properties of steam. Steam from a shower can not only lead to unwanted frizzing of the hair, but it can also be hazardous to the clinical application of a proper amount of mascara, not to mention the tribulations of applying lip-liner in a foggy mirror. I mean really, what was I thinking? In case you are wondering, showering while she is attempting to use the straightening iron is even worse.

I have also learned that it is not necessary to wait until you have completely run out of a particular product before purchasing more of said item, it turns out that a girl can never have too many different kinds of moisturizer or shampoo, nor is it true that all toners were created equal. I have worn the same cologne for years, never realizing that I may have been selling myself short all along: not only might it not have been my signature fragrance, I have been negligent when it comes to scenting for seasonal change. My spring fragrance now possesses a much lighter citrus topnote, far more appropriate for the weather than my more woodsy winter blend.

Not to mention this news flash: a good facial moisturizer is not optional.

I was going to comment on moving day that she might need to pare down some of the four boxes of bathroom products I packed up our stairs, but then I remembered that she hadn't blinked an eye at my entire truckload of tools, or even inquired as to why I owned three bikes, none of which she had ever seen me actually ride. Before my house fire, I owned eleven pairs of black boots, and she never raised an eyebrow at that, either.

We have a much different approach to home improvement, hers is the 'Why don't we just try this and see if it works' method, as opposed to my 'Let's read three books and consult a professional, and then take the eight-week course' tactic. I wanted to wait until I had time to buy the half-inch bell-hanging drill bit and drill a hole through the wall to properly run the ethernet cable into her room. She waited until I was out teaching a class one night, and tacked the cable along the carpet and across the stairs instead. I couldn't even complain that it was unsightly, because I walked right over it without noticing, largely due to the fact that she had painted the cable the exact same colour as the rug with low-gloss nail polish. Now we don't have to bring paint swatches home to match colours to the carpet, we can just bring the bottle of "London Bridge Is Falling Brown" straight to General Paint, saving us yet another superfluous and time-consuming step.

Since the old pipe connected to the shower in the bathroom was rusted and its threads were welded to the old leaking showerhead, I mistakenly believed that installing the new detachable one was going to be a big job. I was pretty sure that we were going to have to knock out a couple of tiles to get at the old pipe and replace it, and that while we were at it we might as well re-do all the tiles as well. I had completed the preliminary research and signed us both up for the tile workshop at the Home Depot, and then I had to go on tour for a couple of days. When I got home there was a gleaming new silver showerhead installed. She had bypassed the old shower altogether, and just removed the main faucet and attached the hose for the new shower to that pipe instead. The old shower now provides a nice place to hang that puffy pink bath-scrubber thingy from.

I have learned that the right way to do things is often the long way to do things, and that sometimes the long way doesn't get done.

We also have a lot of common interests, which is one

of the reasons I think we co-habitate so successfully; our shared love of cigarettes, all foods made of meat, and Air Supply, to name but a few. We both believe in the importance of a clean bathroom, Sunday dinner, and the morning paper.

Sure, living with my girlfriend has cut back on my ability to bring home lap-dancers in the middle of the night, but those kinds of activities always turned out to be more complicated than they initially appeared to be anyway, and often more trouble than they were worth.

I can still work in my underwear, but I hardly ever eat soup right out of the pot anymore. It seems a little gauche now, what with the new table and the floral arrangements and all. Besides, it marks up the coasters.

Pushing Forty

I keep thinking if I ignore it long enough, it will just go away. I keep telling myself that I can't possibly be lactose intolerant, on account of how much I love cheese, and ice cream, and drinking milk right out of the carton. I figure if I just persevere, and just make sure to have a little dairy every day, that slowly I will build up an immunity again, and it will all be good.

Adult onset allergies, my doctor tells me, are more common these days than ever, a combination of pollution, stress, immune systems weakened by antibiotics; I'm not alone, she tells me, she sees it all the time.

This doesn't make me feel any better, this knowing that I have a rather common kind of garden-variety ailment. I'd almost prefer to be debilitated by something a little more rare, something elusive to diagnose and involving a lot less phlegm. Something a little more butch.

My little sister was always the allergic one growing up, along with my mother. Carrie couldn't drink milk or eat strawberries. Her entire childhood was shadowed by a running nose and itchy bouts of hives. My mother's foes were dust and dogs and cats and a certain kind of pollen from an indigenous species of tree, especially in the spring.

Back then, in the seventies, family policy was to just kind of ignore allergies, there were pills you could take I'm sure but no one believed in them, and it was generally implied to us all that those prone to allergies were somehow weaker than the rest of us, or possibly doing it for the attention, or just plain not trying hard enough. Getting rid of the dog or using a soy substitute would only encourage their inconvenient behaviour. Why take it out on the poor pets, or milk and milk products? Why punish the many strong ones and coddle the faulty few?

My mom tells me on the phone that her allergies changed right around the time she was my age, that in her late thirties she developed a whole new batch of intolerances, and that she had to add a multitude of processed food preservatives, penicillin, and sulphates to the already long list of things her body reacted to. "You're just getting old," she told me, like I would find this news comforting.

It still seems bizarre to me, somehow, that foods I have always considered friendly, my body now finds hostile. That someone born and raised in the Yukon could possibly sneeze when exposed to tree pollen. That a former landscaper could develop an intolerance to lawn clippings. That this person could be me. That I could be pushing forty. When did I turn into the person perusing the soymilk selection at the health food store? Where did the lines in my forehead come from, and whose hips are those, anyways?

I was lamenting my ever-increasing hips a couple of days ago to two of my older butch friends. They snorted at me, like I was complaining that I was still too young to buy my own beer.

"Wait till you start to grow the gut," one laughed.

My other friend nodded in sympathy, patting her own belly. "The hip thing slows down once you hit menopause, but then the belly speeds up. What really gets me though, is the turkey skin under my chin. Losing my young neck was the hardest thing for me. That, and my eyesight. Bi-focals are fucking expensive."

Again, I was not comforted.

My mom calls again, this time to inform me that she has recently been diagnosed with Celiac disease, meaning she is now not allowed to eat wheat, rye, barley, spelt ... the list goes on for a frightening long while. She then informs me that this condition is hereditary, and that I need to go get tested myself. She starts bemoaning her imminent divorce from pasta and fresh bread, but I can no longer hear her, the sound of blood rushing in my ears has become too loud. I am imagining myself as one of those people I used to make fun of, the ones who show up for dinner at a friend's house with their own special salad dressing in a Ziploc bag. The ones who interrogate the harried waitress for ten minutes and then end up ordering a miso soup. Wait a second. Will I still be allowed miso soup? Thank Christ I'm not a vegetarian, I think, and then wonder how long a person can actually live without pancakes. If I might eventually go nuts and start snatching handfuls of pasta off of other people's plates when out in public. If I could actually go out in public. All that starch, just taunting me like that. She hangs up, and I Google Celiac disease. The first website that pops up is *www.whats-wrong-with-me.com*. I'm not making this up. Seriously.

Last week I was strolling the drive with my cousin Dan, and we ran into a friend of mine.

"Let's go grab a table at the Roma," she gestures with a toss of her curls. "I'll buy us all a coffee."

Dan and I both look down at our shoes, sheepish. "Neither of us can drink coffee anymore," he says, and I feel a blush creeping from under my collar. "It make us both anxious."

She laughs, secure still in her late twenties. "Well maybe I can buy you both a nice steamed milk, then, maybe with a bit of almond syrup in it."

I cough, my ears on fire now. "Actually, we're both lactose intolerant, too."

"And nuts make my throat swell up," Dan adds. I think he's joking, but I'm not sure.

She shakes her head, just like I used to. "Herbal tea? Organic peppermint?"

I look at my watch, shake my head. "I gotta run. I have to get to the vet before it closes. My little dog needs special prescription food now. He has bladder stones. It's not his fault. He's getting old."

Imagine a Pair of Boots

Imagine a pair of boots. A sturdy, well-made, kind of non-descript pair of boots. They are functional enough, but kind of plain. Imagine that you live in a country where every citizen is issued this one pair of boots at birth, and that there are no other footwear options permitted by law. If you grow out of or wear through the soles of these government-issued boots, you may trade them in for a new pair, always identical to your old ones. Imagine that everyone you know wears these very same boots without question or complaint.

Now imagine that your right foot is two sizes bigger than your left one. That no matter what you do, one boot will chafe and the other will slip, and both will cause blisters. When you mention your discomfort you are told that odd-sized pairs of boots are forbidden, because they cause confusion and excess paperwork. It is explained to you that this footwear system works perfectly for everyone else, and reminded that there are people in other countries who have no boots at all. You are beat up in grade three because none of the other kids have ever seen feet like yours. The teacher tells you that you should probably just learn to keep your boots on. Your parents blame each other. You end up wearing an extra sock on your small foot to compensate, and never go to swimming pools. Your feet sweat profusely in the summer and you always undress in the dark. You hate your feet but need them to walk and stand up on. You hate your boots even more. You dream of things that look like sandals and moccasins, but you have no words for them. You learn things will be easier for you if you just never talk about your feet. One time on the bus, you spot a guy with the exact same limp as you, but you pretend not to see him. He watches you limp off at your bus stop and then looks the other way. You can't stop thinking about the man with the limp for weeks. You are nineteen years old and until that day on the bus you thought you were the only person in the country who couldn't fit into their boots.

I have always felt this way about gender pronouns, that 'she' pinches a little and 'he' slips off me too easily. I'm often asked by well-intentioned people which pronoun I prefer, and I always say the same thing: that I don't really have a preference, that neither pronoun really fits, but thank you for asking, all the same. Then I tell them they can call it like they see it, or mix it up a little if they wish. Or, they can try to avoid using he or she altogether. I suggest this even though I am fully aware of the fact it is almost impossible to talk about anything other than yourself or inanimate objects without using a gender specific pronoun. It is especially hard at gigs, when the poor host has to get up and introduce me to the audience. No matter which pronoun the host goes with, there is always someone cringing in the crowd, convinced that an uncomfortable mistake has just been made. I know it would be easier if I just picked a pronoun and stuck with it, but that would be a compromise made for the comfort of everyone else but me. A decision that would inevitably leave me with a blister, or even a nasty rash.

Perfect strangers have been asking me if I am a boy or a girl as far back as I can remember. Not all of them are polite about it. Some are just curious, others ask me like they have every right to know, as if my ambiguity is a personal insult to their otherwise completely understandable reality. Few of them seem to realize they have just interrupted my day to demand I give someone I don't know personal information they don't really need to sell me a movie ticket or a newspaper. I have learned the hard way to just answer the question politely, so they don't think I'm rude. In my braver days, when someone asked if I was a boy or a girl, I would say something flip and witty, like 'yes' or 'no' or 'makes you wonder, doesn't it?,' but I found that this type of tactic greatly increased the chances I would get the living shit kicked out of me, so I eventually knocked it off. Then I went through a phase where I would answer calmly, and then casually ask them something equally as personal, such as did they have chest hair or were they satisfied with the size of their penis or were those their real breasts, just so they would see how it felt, but this proved just as ineffective.

A couple of months ago, as I was smoking outside the Anza Club after a gig, this young guy marched up and interrupted the person I was talking with to ask me if I was a man or a woman. I told him I was a primarily estrogen-based organism, and then I asked him the exact same question. He took two steps back and dropped his jaw.

"I'm a man." He seemed visibly shaken by the thought of any other option.

"And were you just born male?" I continued, winking at my companion.

"Well, yeah, of course I was."

"How interesting." I lit another smoke.

"Hard to tell these days," my friend chimed in.

The guy walked off, looking confused and kind of vulnerable.

"He's gone home to grow a moustache," my buddy said, then laughed and shook his head.

I thought about it all later, how the guy's ego had crumpled right in front of us, just because a stranger had questioned his masculinity. How scared he was of not being a real man, how easy it had been to take him down. It dawned on me that if you've never had a blister, then you'll never have a callous, either. And if your soles are too soft, then you are fucked if you ever lose your boots.

The Bathroom Chronicles

Lately, I find myself on the road a lot. Sleeping in beds unfamiliar with the shape of me, feeling along strange walls to find the light switch in the dark, waking up to wonder at a ceiling I've never seen before in the daylight of a different town. Wearing the same pair of pants for a week and running my fingers over a calling card in my pocket when I miss my girlfriend. Airports and a highway and little tiny soaps and MapQuest and gas stations. Always gas stations. Because no matter where you are, or how much time you have until you have to be somewhere else, you're going to need gas, and someone always has to pee.

For me, the best gas station bathroom scenario is the single stall version with the sturdy locking door with a sign on it that says men-slash-women and you don't have to ask for the key first. These are the bathrooms most conducive to a stress-free urination experience for me, for a number of reasons. First of all, you don't need to ask for the key. The key for the gas station bathroom is usually somewhat wet for some reason, which I find unsanitary and disturbing, and is invariably tied or chained to a filthy germ-harbouring item which is hard to pocket or lose, such as a piece of hockey stick, a giant spoon, or a tire iron. You have to ask for the key from the either bored or harried and always underpaid guy behind the counter, and if there are two keys, one for the men's and another for the women's, then the cashier has either no time if there's a line-up, or lots of time if things are slow, to decide for himself which key he should give you. Keep in mind that he is probably feeling unfulfilled about the fact that he is ten times more likely to be robbed at gunpoint than he is to get a raise anytime in the near future, and that deciding which washroom he thinks I should be using is the most arbitrary power he's been afforded by this job since he caught that twelve-year-old shoplifting condoms and decided not to call the cops because at least the kid was stealing responsibly.

So this is the guy who gets to decide where I get to pee. I have learned that asking for the key to a specific washroom will only increase the odds that he will notice that the washroom I wish to enter doesn't match the hair or voice or footwear of the person he sees in front of him. Maybe he couldn't give a fuck which bathroom I use, maybe his favourite sister is a dyke. But maybe his religion tells him I am damned, maybe him and his buddies almost killed a guy once for wearing a pink shirt, just in case he was a queer, just for fun. Maybe he dreamt of kissing his best friend all the way through grade eight but never did, and he hates me because I remind him of how scared he is of his own insides. I cannot know his mind. I am in a strange town, and something about me doesn't fit. It is best if I let him decide, and don't draw attention, or alert anyone in the line-up behind me to his conundrum.

Maybe you think I'm just paranoid, that I'm a drama queen, or that I exaggerate to make a point. I would say good for you, that your gender or skin colour or economic status have allowed you to feel safe enough that you still think the rest of us are making this stuff up. You probably don't even realize how lucky you are to be able to not believe me when I tell you that every time I have to pee in a public bathroom, I also take a risk that someone will take issue with me being somewhere they believe to be the wrong room, depending on who they mistook me to be, based solely on that first quick glance.

I can pray for a wheelchair-accessible stall, or one of the ungendered kind with a baby-changing station in it, and then hope that no one is waiting there when I slip out, able-bodied and childless. I can cross my fingers that the ladies' room is empty, or bolt quietly for the closest empty stall if it is not. Unfortunately, women and children have many good reasons to fear what they think is a man in their washroom. I have learned to be more forgiving of their concern, and try not to take any hostility too personally. They only want the same thing I'm looking for: a safe place to pull down their pants and pee.

I can hold my nose and use the men's room, and if I'm lucky there will be a seat on the toilet and the guy who comes in to use the urinal will not be the type who hates slightly effeminate men, or the type who likes them a little too much. In men's rooms, I squat and pee quickly, simultaneously relieved and terrified when I am alone.

Over the years I have learned a few techniques, like not drinking pop in movie theatres and holding my pee for probably unhealthy lengths of time. I do my best to be polite and non-confrontational, even when confronted or questioned rudely. One of my favourite methods is to enter the women's room with a preferably ladylike companion who has been previously instructed to ask me if I have a tampon in my purse. I answer her in the most demure and feminine tone I can muster that I left my purse in the car, or that I'm down to my last pantyliner, and dash for the first open stall.

Just recently, I accidentally improvised the perfect line to deliver to the nice but confused lady that I often meet on my way out of the gas station bathroom. She was standing with her hand on the half-open door, looking first at me and then again at the sign that said "Women" on it. She was in her later sixties, and I felt bad that I had startled her, or maybe made her feel even for a moment that she was lost, or in the men's room, where she might not be safe. That I had scared an old woman with a full bladder. Again.

"It's okay," I smiled and said calmly. "It's just me."

Thicker Than Water

Everybody always says I look just like him. Every once in a while, my grandmother hauls out the second oldest photo album from her closet and opens it on the kitchen table, next to the cut crystal bowl of sugar cubes and the matching cup that holds the little silver teaspoons. She slides the teapot aside to make room and squints over her bifocals. If I have brought a friend with me, this is the part where she makes them try to pick out which face in the faded black-and-white photos belongs to my father. My dad has three brothers. They are wearing matching plaid shirts, or bathing suits, or cub scout uniforms, or hand-me-down pajamas and holsters for their cap guns. In the background there is a Christmas tree, or a lopsided front porch, or a wall tent, or a brass statue of a war hero from the summer the old man took them to Winnipeg to see the army base and learn some respect for the soldiers who fought and died so the rest of us could sit around in our underwear and read comic books and not eat the peas or the broccoli he worked all day to pay good money for. It is always easy to find my dad's face in the photographs. I look just like him, but without the ears. My grandmother named him Don, after his father, she tells my friend. This is the part where if it is raining or her knees are bad she will confess that she never really loved the old bastard, that he was never half the man his sons turned out to be.

More and more, I find little bits of my father in me. Not

just around the eyes or in the shape of my jaw, but how I can't stand to have less than half a tank of gas in my car, because you never know. How I hate cheap tools and dull knives and loose screws. How I own twenty pairs of the exact same underwear. How I can't stop looking for something until I find it, even when I'm late, even if I don't need it until the day after tomorrow. I have to know where it is. My smokes are always in my left pocket, lighter in the right. I can't sleep if the dishes aren't done, can't read only half of a book, and I never turn off the radio until the song is over. I like a little bit of egg, potato, and bacon in every bite of my breakfast. It is a finely tuned ratio, constantly being weighed and adjusted throughout the meal. Nothing worse than winding up with only hashbrowns in the end. Always let your engine warm up before you drive anywhere and cool down a bit before you turn it off. You can double the life of a motor if you treat it right. Driving fast burns more gas and is hard on your brake pads. Besides, you just spend more time waiting for the light to turn green. Don't go grocery shopping on an empty stomach. All of these things I learned from my father. Most of the time I do them without thinking of him, but every once in a while I remember; these are inherited habits. Other fathers might have saved their bacon until last, or ran out of gas, or hired someone else to build their house. Other fathers might have worn dress shoes to work instead of steel-toed boots. A different kind of dad might not have taught me how to weld. A man with sons might not have let his daughter drive the forklift.

Who would I be if he had been someone else?

A couple of months ago, I had a gig in Calgary. An all-queer spoken word show at a sports bar downtown, right in the middle of the hockey playoffs. Strange, but true. I was wearing a dark blue shirt with thin stripes, and a sky blue tie that subtly highlighted the secondary tones of my shirt. The waitress liked my stories and kept slipping me free scotch on the rocks after the show, and I had about four stiff drinks in me when this huge guy in a Flames jersey grabbed me by the necktie and pulled my nose right into his chest hair.

"Your tie is all fucked up. Where'd you learn that? Nobody ever taught you how to do a proper double Windsor? Fuckin' disgrace. Come here, lemme show you."

I tried to explain that I had been drinking, and was thus unable to engage in activities that required concentration or hand-eye co-ordination, plus it was dark and my tie was fine anyway, but he pulled my substandard knot loose and laid a drunken death grip on my right shoulder.

"I'm in the fucking Mafia. The fucking Mafia knows how to tie a tie. You going to argue how to tie a tie with the Mafia, or you going to shut up and watch me do this right?"

I mentioned that I had read somewhere that the real Mafia never admits that there is a real Mafia, and that Calgary wasn't known for being a hotbed of organized crime, and that the odds were neither of us would remember any of this in the morning anyway, but he insisted.

I ended up getting a nonconsensual thirty-minute lesson in proper manly attire from a guy with one leg of his track pants accidentally tucked into his white sweat sock. He started with the double Windsor knot demonstration and went on to sum up the billfold versus money clip conundrum for me. He was pontificating on the merits of French cuffs when his buddy interrupted to announce they were all leaving to go catch the peelers.

I woke early the next morning, dry-mouthed and blurry. I pulled a clean shirt and a different tie out of my suitcase and was amazed when my fingers remembered what tying a perfect double Windsor knot felt like. I don't remember who taught me the wrong way to tie a tie, but I know for sure it wasn't my dad. He never wears neckties. He taught me how to tie a boat to a dock, and a fishhook to a line. How to tie double bows in your bootlaces so they never come undone halfway down a ladder or get caught up in a conveyor belt or a lawnmower blade and end up costing you a toe. My father is a wise man. He taught me all the important knots. The double Windsor I learned from a wise guy.

Hot For Freezer

I can't pinpoint exactly where it all changed. I know the house fire had a lot to do with it: nothing will feng shui your life faster or more thoroughly than an old-fashioned, six-hour inferno, and nothing makes you re-think your relationship to material possessions quite like losing them all. But even that aside, my priorities are all different now.

I haven't replaced my assless chaps, and I no longer dream of owning an old BSA motorcycle. Instead, I salivate over my neighbour's refinished hardwood floors and get hard-ons walking through the stainless steel appliance section at The Bay.

A couple of weeks ago, I was standing in line at the Home Depot when I realized that I was kind of alarmingly excited about the brand new weed whacker and 5.5 cubic foot deep-freeze I was about to purchase. And I wasn't the only one. The thirtysomething couple behind me caught sight of the shiny black mini-freezer on my cart, and the woman elbowed her mate.

"Look, honey. Maybe if you got rid of some of your boxes from the back porch and organized your golf clubs better, we could make room for one of those."

He shook his head. "They draw too much power. It would probably constantly kick the breaker."

"Actually, this baby only draws about point two amps, continuous service," I said, surprised at how proud I sounded. "I've done all the research already. You don't even need a dedicated circuit, provided you locate the unit close enough to an outlet so an extension cord is not required," I continued, assuming they were just as fascinated as I was.

She was, he wasn't.

"Voltage drop," I explained.

She nodded, he didn't.

The freezer was actually a birthday present for my girlfriend who is a Cancer, and thus appreciates all things domestic. Not everyone can recognize the inherent romance of having frozen bacon-wrapped scallops on hand anytime, or the sexiness of saving money by buying in bulk, but she does. My mother was horrified to hear that I was getting my sweetheart a deep freeze for her birthday, but my mom doesn't truly understand how important ice cream is to my girl's general outlook. Not to mention her love of homemade soup. I knew that a deep freeze would revolutionize my household's access to quality late-night snacks, and for a Cancer, that is romantic. My mom is a Virgo, and therefore is more turned on by cleaning products or a well-designed closet organizer.

Each to their own, I say. One man's assless chaps are another man's self-feeding weed whacker with ergonomic handgrips and a built-in lock to keep the extension cord from coming unplugged. I could hardly wait to get home and slip into my matching eye protection.

Like I said, I can't pinpoint exactly where it all changed, but somewhere in the last couple of years things shifted and now I would rather plant perennials than party, and thumbing through the Restoration Hardware catalogue has become my new pornography. Egyptian cotton sheets are, well ... hot.

Before my house fire, I wasn't bothered by my mismatched dishes, or the fact that most of my cutlery had the Air Canada logo engraved on the handles. But there was something different about rebuilding the contents of a kitchen in my late thirties instead of my late teens. For a while there I even worried that I was slowly turning into an insufferable yuppie, that I was more concerned with making sure my tea towels matched the countertops than I was with making the world a better place. Until my friend reminded me that if I were truly a yuppie, then I would have sought out a more lucrative occupation than being a queer Canadian writer, and that investing in quality cookware was actually an environmentally responsible life choice. He went on to add that landfills all over the continent were full of broken low-quality consumer goods, and that saving up for the copper-bottomed pots and pans didn't necessarily mean I had become an unrepentant capitalist.

"It's easier to fight for gay rights and social change if you're not dying from cancer caused by cooking in a pan treated with a substandard spray-on non-stick coating," he reassured me. "You're just thinking of the big picture, here. Besides, you can write more if you treat yourself to the really fluffy bath towels. They're more absorbent. It's a time-saver."

A shallow justification, maybe, but it worked. Our towels now highlight the stripes in the shower curtain, and the little scented soaps that we keep on top of the toilet tank, the ones we don't use, because they are matching. And I refuse to be ashamed that I like it that way.

I am an unapologetic butch who refuses to conform to anyone's definition of what gender I am, and I write decidedly queer stories about people who dare to be proud of who and what we are, even in a world that still for the most part despises or denies that we exist. And that means I am still a warrior, even though the blinds in my bedroom window are the exact same shade of brown as the bedspread. It's more of a cinnamon colour than a chocolate, and it really picks up the secondary tones in the area rug. And I like it that way.

Like I said, one man's pornography is another man's brass reading lamp with the articulated adjustable arm and three-way light bulb.

Whatever turns you on.

Judging a Book

There's an old cliché, something about how you can choose your friends but you can't choose your family. I travel a lot, and I'd like to add a line, or at least a footnote, about how you also can't choose who you sit next to on an airplane ride, especially if you're flying in economy class.

I am a collector of stories, and a connoisseur of characters, so for the most part I love the random way that travelling strangers enter and exit each other's lives. I relish the chance to spend a few hours listening to the life story of a little old lady who usually only talks to her cat or the postman, or the girl that her family hired to come and clean the house once a week, ever since her daughter got too busy with the twins and the promotion. I notice how thin her skin seems, stretched like tracing paper over the blue veins that map the backs of her hands. How they shake just a little when she holds up a photo for me to see, how she spills a little bit of sugar when she pours it from the tiny packet and has to hold her paper cup with both hands. I savour all these details, and save them as souvenirs. Some people take pictures or buy postcards to remember where they have been. I collect people, and conversations.

One time I spent three hours waiting for the fog to lift in San Francisco with a guy who told me that he spends so much time on the road he never fully unpacks his suitcase, and that he has missed nine of his son's twelve birthday parties. He was a salesman who had single-handedly cornered the North American market for snow globes. His chest swelled proudly when he passed me his business card and announced that if I ever bought a quality snow globe anywhere on the continent, chances were it was one of his. Not the cheap ones, mind you, but the good kind, where the snow floats around for a while before it falls and collects on the bottom.

When he found out I was a writer, he told me he had spent the last ten years working on a novel, mostly at night in hotel rooms, and that when he finally retired, he was going to take a screenwriting class.

"Maybe I'm a writer too," he told me. "You never know. Stranger things have happened."

I told him I thought everyone had at least 1,000 great stories to tell, but we have been taught to believe that only heroes or serial killers or rich people or crime scene investigators live lives worth writing down. He rubbed his bald spot with one hand for a bit, like he was thinking about something he forgot to do, and took a deep breath.

That's when he blurted out that he hated his job, but the only thing he'd ever been better than everyone else at was selling snow globes, and that his wife hadn't touched him in three years, ever since he put on forty pounds after his back surgery, and he was pretty much convinced that she was banging his son's soccer coach and how the worst part was that he didn't even care anymore, but he didn't want to leave her because she would get the house, and he loved that house, and his dog, who had lived to be almost fifteen year old, was buried in the backyard right next to the apple tree, and what if his wife sold the house and bought a condo when the kids moved out so she wouldn't have to mow the lawn, and maybe a dead dog was a terrible reason to stay married to someone who won't look at you without a shirt on, but he was hardly ever home anyways, except for long weekends like this, and if the weather didn't get better he wouldn't make it home at all. Then he apologized and said he didn't know why he was telling me all this, that he hadn't even talked to his best friend about any of it, on account of how they worked for the same company, and getting too personal might put a strain on their business relationship. I hugged a perfect stranger that night because I knew his wife wouldn't, and I think of him now whenever I see snow that falls slowly.

Today I sat next to a man who immediately informed me that he was on his way to Europe to work with the Christian Embassy, spreading the good word of the Lord. Before the plane was off the ground, he asked me if I had a girlfriend. I took this line of inquiry to mean that he thought I was a clean-cut young man, and therefore possessed a soul worth saving. I told him the truth; I did have a girlfriend, and no, we were not married yet, and yes, we were indeed living together, and yes, I was aware that we were living in sin. I smiled inside at just how much sin he didn't realize we were actually living in, and pondered telling him I was not as nice, young, or male as he appeared to think I was. Then I realized how fun it was to listen to a fundamentalist Christian lecture me on how God wanted me to marry my girlfriend, how the family unit in this country was depending on me, and how not fun it might immediately become if he were to find out he was brushing thighs with a full-blown sodomite disguised as a harmless wayward Catholic boy in a crisp shirt and a tie. I knew there was as much chance of me changing his mind about anything as there was that he would ever lead me back to the path of righteousness, so I told him he was right, and that I was going to propose to my girlfriend as soon as I had enough money saved up to buy her a decent conflict-free diamond ring. He took this to mean that he had helped me see the light, and continued the Lord's work all the way to Toronto. When the plane finally landed, he shook my hand and told me that I seemed like a good person, and that if I were ever in Guelph, I should look up his son, who had strayed from God's path a little and had pierced his eyebrow and was pursuing an arts degree.

"I'd like him to meet some friends with ambition. People who realize that appearances matter. I pray that he grows up to be just like you."

"I hope God answers that prayer," I told him. "I really do."

How I Knew

Looking back, I'd have to say I knew right away that she was something special. I can't remember the exact series of events that resulted in our first date consisting of shooting beer cans with a pellet gun in the garage with my friends, but I will never forget that she wore a pink turtleneck sweater. I was also impressed that her high-heeled boots didn't seem to impair her ability to handle a gun at all.

Most surprising, of course, was that she agreed to go out with me a second time. I was recently single and therefore skeptical, and reluctant to waste time dating anyone who might not appreciate my new hobbies, which were classic rock, cooking steaks, and chain smoking. I told her that I would love to have her over for dinner, as long as she wasn't a vegan. She laughed on the other end of the phone and I heard her light up a cigarette.

"Vegan? You've got to be kidding me. I'm Danish. Our national dish is, like, two kinds of meat, wrapped in meat."

Later that night she ran her fingers lazily through my hair, our four legs a naked tangle, lipstick on my pillow, sheets in a twist on the floor. She whispered into the dark.

"I'm not looking to get involved with anyone, really. My theory is that most of the magic happens in the first three months. I plan to have as much fun with you as I can for the next ninety days or so, and then get out while the getting is good. Before we have to process anything, or talk about house keys, or monogamy. Before you meet my mother."

At the time, and given my circumstances, this seemed impossibly romantic.

Six weeks later, my house burned down.

Maybe she thought it would be cruel to dump someone who had no furniture or dishes and only three pairs of socks; I've never asked. But my ninety days came and then went, and she didn't. By that time, I had taken to smelling the clothes she left at my new house when she wasn't around and playing the same song twenty times in a row and buying three giant bottles of that raspberry lemonade she seemed to like.

Her mother loved me, even though I was ripped on muscle relaxants the first time I met her. I lied and said I threw my back out moving a couch because the truth involved her daughter, a pair of pantyhose, and vanilla-scented massage oil.

The night I introduced her to my family, my mother said that she had never seen me happier, and my uncle grabbed me by the elbow and dragged me into his guest room and closed the door.

"Don't you fuck this one up," he warned me. "She's the one, I can feel it. The whole family loves her. She's gorgeous, and she can cook. She even likes fishing. Don't be an idiot. Marry her already."

It was true. Not only did she like road trips and divey motels and beef dips and drip coffee and smalltown AM radio, she also loved to fish. One time, my uncle took us out on the lake in his boat, and I saw the way her eyes lit up when she landed her first lake trout. He noticed it too, and raised both eyebrows in a meaningful fashion at me and nodded his approval when she wasn't looking.

This is one quality babe, his eyebrows had said. *Don't play catch and release with this one.*

By the time we moved in together last fall, I was well and truly smitten. Love songs and long-distance commercials could bring me to tears, and I would willingly give her the last doughnut, the last of the hot water, the last word. For the first time in my life, I was actually paying attention to the latest developments in the gay marriage debate.

She makes me want to stand up in front of all my friends and relatives and say, "I pick her, and she picks me. She likes fishing and Air Supply, and I love the smell of her neck. I want to buy her a house with enough closet space, and have dinner ready when she gets home from work. I want to mow the lawn and fold her socks, amen."

We haven't set an actual date. We're still trying to decide whether we want a circus theme or a sports day-inspired wedding. I maintain there is no real reason that we can't have stilt-walkers and three-legged races at the same event. I mean, it is a gay wedding, who needs to stand on ceremony? My uncle Dave the renegade Catholic priest said he would do the honours, and all my best men will be women. I figure the beauty of gay marriage is that we get to choose which traditions we want to honour, and then make the rest up as we go along. We're definitely serving Danish meatballs at the reception. We're registering at Lee Valley Tools and Home Depot. No one is giving either of us away, and all of our ex-lovers are invited. I'm buying her a diamond engagement ring, but we're going to exchange filet knives instead of wedding bands. Formal dress is requested, and all guests will be encouraged to bring their own sleeping bags, swimwear, and bug repellent. There will be a live band, a complimentary bar, and waterskiing. It will be the dream wedding that neither of us ever dreamed we'd dream of having. Afterwards, we're going to honeymoon in either Cache Creek or Costa Rica, depending on the weather, and the fishing.

Just In Case

The first time I really knew for sure was the summer I turned six. If you were to ask either of my parents, both of them would probably blame the other, each of them for entirely different reasons, but I like to think I was just born this way.

Looking back it is obvious that I had shown signs much earlier, subtle symptoms and certain tendencies that had gone unnoticed. But somewhere in the summer that stretched between being five and turning six, I grew up enough to realize that I wasn't like the other kids. It all started with my dad's new truck, a second-hand Chevy. Robin's egg blue, with navy and cream vinyl interior, and an 8-track bolted under the dashboard. Chrome bumpers that flashed silver in the sun, winking diamonds of light when the truck swung around the corner. You could see your face in the chrome; it bent and stretched reflections like a circus mirror. But what I remember most was the winch, and how it changed everything.

If you look up the word winch in the dictionary, it will tell you it is a hauling or lifting device consisting of a rope or chain winding around a horizontal rotating drum, turned typically by a crank or motor. My dad's new pick-up had a winch mounted right on the front grill, just above the bumper. It was made of steel and smelled like oil and rust.

You could do a lot with a winch, he told me. You could

tie it to a tree and pull yourself out of a ditch. Drag heavy objects. Rescue people who got their car stuck in mud, sand, or snow. A guy could maybe even save somebody's life one day, you never knew, just because he happened to come upon a drastic situation where somebody was in dire need of a winch. The thought of helping my father save the day with a winch both thrilled and terrified me.

One thing that nobody knew about me was that I spent a great deal of time thinking about disasters. This usually occurred at night just before sleep took over, at which time I would dream of calamities. My grandmother had unknowingly planted the seed of potential danger in my imagination when she taught me the common bedtime prayer recited by generations of Catholic children: Now I lay me down to sleep, I pray the Lord my soul to keep, and if I should die before I wake, I pray the Lord my soul to take. Then she would turn the light off and leave us in the dark. Of course, this prayer begged the question of just how death might sneak up on a sleeping child, so I would lay there, sweat sticking my skin to my pajamas, waiting for a plane to crash through the roof, wondering if bears could open doors, or if there was something under the bed. Worrying about lightning, tornadoes, or sometimes poisoned apples. In the early days of kindergarten, a fireman came to our school and taught us to stop, drop and roll if we ever caught on fire, and hide under our desks in case of an earthquake. I didn't have a desk at home, and so I barely slept for the next three nights, until I discovered I was still small enough to fit inside my bedside table, if I moved the humidifier and took the little drawer all the way out. For Christmas that year, I asked Santa for my very own fire extinguisher and a first aid kit. I had realized something about myself. I wasn't really afraid of the dark or the sight of my own blood. What terrified me were flashlights with dead batteries, or when someone used the last band-aid and put the empty box back into the drawer without telling anyone. It wasn't what might happen that scared me. It was not being ready for it that kept me up at night. Knowing I had access to a winch if I needed one brought me great comfort. So did swimming lessons, where we learned to tread water and give mouth-to-mouth resuscitation.

Last week, my sweetheart and I got caught in a snow-storm driving home from Seattle. A giant tree had fallen across the highway and trapped us in the middle of miles of motionless cars and trucks. Wind whipped and branches bent and swirling snowflakes strangled what was left of the daylight.

There were abandoned vehicles everywhere, some nose-first in the ditches, even more half-buried and littering the exits. The guy on the radio was advising everyone to stay off the roads, but had little advice for those of us who were stuck on them.

I did what I have always done when staring down a potential emergency: I took inventory. I had filled up the gas tank just before we left Seattle, so we had plenty of fuel. We had a cellphone complete with charger, and a transformer that plugged in to the cigarette lighter. The storage container on the roof was full of camping gear, so we had blankets, sleeping bags, a Coleman stove, propane, pots, coffee, tea, sugar, and canned milk. In the trunk, I had a shortwave radio and spare batteries, a down jacket, and wool socks. My friends like to tease me about my Ford Taurus station wagon, until they go camping with me. I'm always the only guy who remembers to bring a battery-operated latté whipper. I watched the other drivers slide and skid and spin their tires. They gripped their steering wheels, lips tight and knuckles white. They looked scared.

I reached across the seat to grab my sweetie's hand. While we were in Seattle, we had picked up a little something I had been looking for for a while. It was a portable shower unit that ran on propane. You put one end of the hose into a lake or river, fired it up, and toasty hot water came out the other end. I smiled to myself. Everything was going to be just fine.

Up Here

If you were to leave Vancouver and travel 2,697 kilometres to the northwest, you would be in Whitehorse, Yukon, a little city of 23,272 souls spread out on or around the Yukon River. This is where I grew up. If you were to leave White-horse and travel another 536 kilometres to the northwest, you would find yourself in Dawson City, a much littler city of 1,781 folks clustered into a corner where the Yukon River meets the Klondike. This is where I am living for the month of January. Peace and quiet. A lot of time to write. A lot of time to think. A lot of time to think.

The sun came up at 11:16 a.m. today, and will disappear again at 3:38 p.m. Dawson was built in the shelter and shadow of the Midnight Dome, a peak that looms 2,911 feet above the town. The Dome offers a great view of the land-scape it surveys, but it also blocks any direct sunlight from striking the faces of Dawsonites for most of the winter. There is a glowing patch of mountainside on the southwest edge of town where the afternoon sun manages to slide around the side of the Dome and light up the pine trees and snow for a while. I like to watch this little patch of sunlight stretch and spread like butter across the horizon. I imagine that if I were to trek across the frozen river and crunch through the snow to the sunny spot, it would be warm up there. This is an illusion. It is minus 26 degrees Celsius to-day, and when the sun disappears for another twenty hours, it will drop to minus 38.

Going outside is a bit of a production. I can see the only gas station in town through the frost-flowered window in the kitchen, but to get there I have to don wool socks, long johns, jeans, a T-shirt, a long-sleeved wool shirt, my parka, a neckwarmer, a fur hat with ear flaps, the moosehide mitts my mom got me for Christmas, and my newfangled snow boots. They're a lot lighter than your classic Sorrel skidoo boots but almost as toasty. My gran calls this bundling up, and to me it's like wrapping my head up in memories of my childhood: my own breath, warm and wet, trapped under my nose by the taste of wool, the whistle of parka sleeves and snowpants, the dry squeaking complaint of northern snow announcing every footstep.

People in parkas are pretty much genderless. Parkas cover up curves and boobs, or lack thereof. Scarves and toques mask moustaches or plucked eyebrows. Mittens hide a manicure or hair on the backs of hands. Bundled up, we are all the same. This affords me a strange kind of freedom. When I walk into the grocery store in my cold weather ensemble, the old woman behind the cash register can't tell that my hair doesn't fit my voice, or that my hips don't belong on the body of a teenage boy. I am a stranger, but other than being new in town, there is nothing strange about me. I am dressed for the cold, just like everybody else.

Today we went to a fur show. Urban lesbians, this is not what you are thinking. I'm talking about pelts. Beaver, sable, fox, wolverine, wolf, coyote, and lynx furs, all spread out on folding tables in the community centre gymnasium to be judged based on thickness and colour. The whole town was there; you could barely find a parking spot on Front Street. Mountains of parkas piled up on empty chairs and packs of little kids screeching and sliding around on the gym floor in their sock feet. Free moose stew and bannock, plus all the Tang and drip coffee you could drink. Door prizes and a fur fashion show. The whole nine yards. A guy from the Fur Harvester's Association gave me a bumper sticker that said, 'Kids Who Hunt, Trap and Fish Don't Mug Little Old Ladies.' I tried to imagine some of my vegan friends from the city here, sitting stricken on a chair in the corner, trying not to breathe in the almost overwhelming smell of freshly tanned hides. It would be hard to argue against the merits of wearing fur when it is forty below outside. A lot of big city politics might die of exposure halfway through a Yukon winter.

I've cut back on my cigarette smoking quite a bit, what with the weather outside and not being allowed to smoke inside and all. This gives me a great get-rich-quick idea: I could rent a house in Dawson in the dead of winter and open a Quit Smoking retreat. People could pay good money to come here for two weeks and stay in my very non-smoking bed and no breakfast. I would provide them with thin nylon windbreakers and open-toed slippers, and if they were desperate, they would be more than welcome to smoke outside on the uncovered, unheated deck, conveniently located on the windy side of the residence. I run my new plan past a friend of mine over a dinner of rice pasta and tomato sauce with caribou meatballs. She is convinced that this scheme won't work, that the real nicotine addicts would gladly freeze their asses off instead of going without a ciga-rette. I concede that maybe my plan has a few kinks that I have to work out. I will need to think on it all some more. Fortunately, I have a lot of time to think. Seriously, a lot of time to think.

The Future of Francis

The first time I wrote about my little friend Francis, the little boy who liked to wear dresses, he was three years old. The middle son of one of my most beloved friends, he was the fearless fairy child who provided me with living, pirouetting proof that gender outlaws are just born like that, even in cabins in the bush with no running water or satellite television. He confirmed my theory that some of us come out of the factory without a box or with parts that don't match the directions that tell our parents how we are supposed to be assembled. Watching Francis grow up taught me that what makes him and me different was not bred into us by the absence of a father figure or a domineering mother, or being exposed to too many show tunes or power tools at an impressionable stage in our development. We are not hormonal accidents, evolutional mistakes, or created by a God who would later disown us. Most of us learn at a very early age to keep our secret to ourselves, to try to squeeze into clothes that feel like they belong on someone else's body, and hope that the mean kids at school don't look at us long enough to find something they feel they need to pound out of us. But Francis had a mother who let him wear what he wanted, and Francis had evidence that he was not alone, because Francis had me.

He is eleven now, and I got to hang out with him and his brothers last January, up in Dawson City. He doesn't wear dresses anymore, and I didn't see much of his younger self in the gangly boy body he is growing into. He is a tough guy now, too cool to hug me when his friends are around, full of wisecracks and small-town street smarts. He can ride a unicycle, juggle, and do head spins. He listens to hip-hop and is not afraid to get in a fist fight. He calls other kids faggot, just like his friends do, but only when his mother can't hear him.

I can't help but wonder if the politics of public school have pushed him to conform, or if he has just outgrown his cross-dressing phase and become as butch a son as any father could hope for. I try to imagine what it would be like for him to be the only boy in a dress on a playground full of kids whose parents are trappers and hunters. To be labelled queer in a town of 1,700 people and more than its fair share of souls who survived residential schools, families with four generations of inherited memories of same-sex touches that left scars and shame and secrets. I don't blame him for hiding his difference here, for fighting to fit in.

I walk past his school one day on my way to buy groceries, and watch him kick a frozen soccer ball around in the snow with his buddies. He sees me and stands still for a second, breathing silver clouds of steam into the cold. When he was little, he used to fling himself out his front door when I came to visit and jump on me before I was all the way out of my truck. He would wrap his whole body around my neck and hips and whisper wet secrets and slobber kisses into my ear. Now, he barely returns my wave before he turns and disappears into a sea of snowsuits and scarf-covered faces. I find myself searching the crowd for a boy I barely recognize, a Francis who has outgrown my memory of him. I miss the Francis he used to be, the boy-girl who confessed to me when he was five years old that I was his favourite uncle because we were the same kind of different. Now, I can't tell him apart from all the other boys wearing blue parkas.

I realize later I am doing to Francis exactly what I wish the whole world would stop doing to our children: wanting him to be something he is not, instead of just allowing him to be exactly what he is. I don't want Francis to spend his lunch break being tormented and beaten up. I remember growing my hair in junior high and wanting everyone to like me, and I will never forget the blond boy from school who walked like a girl, and that time in grade eight someone slammed his face in a locker door and gave him a concussion because he wanted to try out for the cheerleading team. By grade ten, he had learned to eat his lunch alone in an empty classroom and wear his gym shorts under his jeans instead of braving the boys' change room, but everybody acted like they were his best friend after he shot himself in the head with his stepfather's hunting rifle during spring break the year we all graduated. They hung his school photo up in the hallway, and all the kids pinned paper flowers and rest in peace notes to the wall around his picture, but nobody wrote that they were sorry for calling him faggot or sticking gum in his hair or making fun of how he threw a ball.

I made a silent promise to Francis the day I left Dawson City to always love what he is right now as much as I loved who he was back then. Whether he grows up to become a textbook heterosexual he-man or one day rediscovers his early love for ladies' garments, I will always be his favourite uncle, no matter what he's wearing.

Rat Bastards

The first couple of times I heard the noise above my head, I thought it was raccoons on the roof. It was definitely some kind of four-legged activity of the rodent variety. I took to racing up to the attic with a broom or hockey stick in my hand to give chase, or at least catch a look at my rivals before they scampered off, but I never once caught sight of a raccoon on the roof.

Probably because it wasn't raccoons I was up against; it was squirrels, and they weren't on my roof, they were inside of it. If you think I am an idiot for mistaking the sound of a tiny little squirrel going about its annoying business for the much larger but no less pesky raccoon, then obviously you are lucky enough never to have had an entire extended family of the filthy little rodents take up residence in the ceiling directly above your office.

Now, I was born and raised in the Yukon, and though I have been an urban dweller for some time now, it is quite possible that deep down inside I may still hold onto a few outlooks that are more bush than I would like to believe. The first option that came up for me with regard to my uninvited houseguests was to simply dig out my gun and shoot the little buggers. Not all of them; I'm not a monster or anything. My plan was to just pick off one or two of the leaders, the fattest and most confident-seeming of the brood. The rest of them would hopefully take the hint and seek alternative shelter elsewhere.

But then I made the mistake of mentioning my plan to one of the women who lives in the suite downstairs.

"You will absolutely do no such thing. If you shoot even one single squirrel, I swear I will tell every vegetarian and/or lesbian in all of East Vancouver. Slowly you will become known as the squirrel murderer, and you will eventually be so ostracized that you will never work in this town again."

I stared at her face, searching for any sign that she wasn't completely serious. I couldn't be sure. My career is still in a position such that I can't really afford to risk even a halfhearted part-time PETA boycott, so I reluctantly put my pellet gun away. At least until she and her girlfriend go to Costa Rica this spring or something.

One of the good old boys from up the street spotted me unloading a supposedly more humane live trap out of the back of my car a couple of months ago. I had already briefed him about my rodent problem. He looked confused as he bent down to give my old dog her now expected biscuit from the stash in his coat pocket.

"Thought you were planning to just shoot the little fuckers? Those traps are time-consuming. Plus sometimes if you don't relocate them far enough away, they just come back."

"My downstairs neighbour won't let me," I lamented. "Says she'll tell all the lesbians on me and they will quit coming out to my shows."

He nodded sympathetically, and shrugged silently as if to say, well, what can you do?

"What are you going to do with them once you have them in the trap?"

"I'm gonna put tiny little squirrel-sized blindfolds on them so they can't see where I'm taking them, then I'll drive them over to Queen Elizabeth or Stanley Park or something and I'll let 'em go."

He shook his head sadly. "Then they'll just dig holes in someone else's attic. Become some poor other guy's problem."

I nodded sympathetically, as if to say, well, what can you do?

A sly smile stretched across his face, and he curved one hand like a bracket around the side of his mouth and whispered, "You know, they're way easier to shoot once you've already got them in the trap."

We both laughed for a minute, and then he and his inherited geriatric hound turned and headed slowly for home.

The thing is, I don't hate the squirrels in my attic just because they're noisy and selfish about keeping it down when I'm trying to concentrate and get my work done. I don't just hate them because they dig little holes in the drywall and get plaster dust all over my printer. I don't just hate them because one day last summer I left the window in my office open and came home to find one of them sitting on the keyboard of my laptop. Then he had the gall to give me quite the huffy little attitude when I chased him out the window and tried to knock him out of my flowerbox.

It's the fire hazard that bothers me. Squirrels really like to chew on electrical wires, and many a fine inferno has a fried little critter as a culprit. Already having had one house burn down makes me all the more reluctant to relive the experience.

My downstairs neighbours already think I have possibly unhealthy conspiracy-slash-survivalist sort of end of the world tendencies, just because I once suggested a house meeting to ensure we have at least seventy-two hours' worth of fresh water and non-perishable food supplies in case of a natural disaster.

Then I had to go and reinforce their fears by trying to shoot stuff on the property.

I didn't want to be right, but just before Christmas, one of the rodents finally bit the wrong wire in the wrong place at the right time and bit it for good. It blew the main breaker in our suite and I had to run a temporary extension cord out the back window and plug our deep freeze in downstairs. Until I have time to fix the wiring, and the squirrels, for good. Relax, I'm going to call in a professional, and have him live trap them and relocate them safely out of my range. I love my downstairs neighbours. It's the ones upstairs that have to go.

Something Old, Something New

I was never one of those little girls who dreamed of my wedding day. The lacy white gown, the flower girls, the handsome groom, the silver embossed napkins: I knew at a very early age that none of it was for me.

I come from a large and unusually fertile Catholic family, so there were a lot of weddings to attend. The ladies would get their hair done and buy new dresses, and the men would squeeze themselves into their good blue suits and dusty dress shoes. My Uncle Dave used to be a biker prior to becoming a priest, and before he got up to lead the ceremony he would yank down the sleeves of his robe to hide the faded tattoos on his forearms so he wouldn't ruin the photos or alarm the new in-laws. My Uncle John was always the bartender, and once the reception was in full swing and no one was looking he would slip a quick shot of rum into your Coke if you swore not to blab to anyone or puke on yourself. Weddings were fun, but I never wanted to be the blushing bride. I wasn't even cut out to be a flower girl, and everyone knew it. I ducked when the bride threw her bouquet so it could be caught by someone who wanted it. I liked the cocktail wieners and the Jell-O salad. I enjoyed watching my uncles get drunk enough to dance or hug or arm-wrestle each other, but the love and marriage part never impressed me.

The subject never came up during the half-hearted heterosexual phase of my life, and the girl I finally kissed in my first year of college couldn't pry her closet door open wide enough to tell her best friend the truth about me.

My next girlfriend was a long-winded socialist who informed me that the institution of marriage was a capitalist invention, designed to oppress women and protect the property and profit of the ruling class. Marriage had nothing to do with love and everything to do with power, she told me. I was nineteen and she was forty, so I believed her.

Then I met a black-haired anarchist at a squatter's rights potluck, and really fell in love for the first time. She worked in an organic food warehouse; I was a landscaper and part-time pool cleaner. We were too busy photocopying manifestos and taking back the night and freeing Mumia Abu Jamal to talk about long-term commitment anyway. Besides, everybody knew that marriage was a sexist tool of the patriarchal state, and monogamy was a counter-revolutionary construct used by organized religion to regulate human sexuality.

It is almost impossible for me to believe that twenty years have passed since I kissed my first girl. That we somehow found each other and flirted and fucked without the help of email or cellphones, or even voice mail. Back then, I wouldn't have believed that one day I would be saving up for high-quality cookware and dreaming of my very own mortgage. I never imagined that my writing would pay the bills. Who could have known that twenty years later I would propose to my live-in life partner in a Ford Taurus station wagon while we were stuck in traffic on our way back from getting the Pomeranian groomed, and that both of us would find this romantic.

I knew she was the one right from the get-go. It's like that for us: we fit perfectly, she and I, and it only made sense. She likes the overcooked brownish potato chips and I don't, so I save them for her. She likes the outside slice from the roast beef, and the crusty end piece from the loaf of gluten-free rice and flaxseed bread. Not to mention the fact that she didn't dump me when we found out I have Celiac disease and it's all my fault we have to eat stuff like gluten-free rice and flaxseed bread.

I thought we had the usual 'who would we get to do the honours' conundrum already sorted out, on account of my Uncle Father Dave and all. He has married everyone who is anyone in my family. Why shop it out to a stranger?

Last week, the good father himself was in town to have the battery in his pacemaker replaced, so naturally we took him out for dim sum and asked if we could book him in advance so as to avoid the summer rush. Imagine our shock and dismay when he shook his head sadly and lowered his pork dumpling long enough to inform us that he was already in enough trouble with the bishop as it was, and he would be unable to marry any homosexuals, even his own flesh-and-blood niece, at least until the storm around his most recent religious infraction had time to blow over. Apparently last month he had gone against Catholic doctrines and married a couple who both had MS, even though he was well aware that they could not procreate. Needless to say, he was in no position to risk another holy scolding.

I never dreamed I would one day find myself carefully

drafting a stern letter to the Pope himself. I would never have imagined there would come a day when I wanted a good old-fashioned church wedding just like the ones my mother dragged me to when I was a kid. My younger cousins say they don't get what the big deal is, why can't we just get the Unitarians to do it for us, or maybe just hire a pagan or a Wiccan priestess or a ship's captain or something? What's the difference, they say, a wedding's a wedding, isn't it?

But they're too young to remember the Jell-O salads, the fist fights and the rock 'n' roll-related lower back injuries, and they're too old to need their favourite uncle to slip rum into their sodas. Kids these days.

Teach the Children Well

Every time I do a storytelling gig at a public school, I swear to myself that I will never do it again. I promise myself that this is the last time, that the next time they ask me I will remember that I have decided to avoid attempting to entertain large groups of teenagers for health reasons, that breathing gymnasium air makes me dangerously dehydrated, that hallways lined with lockers can cause painful grade eight flashbacks. High schools remind me of high school, I can't help it. I graduated twenty years ago, but all it takes is the sound of the first period buzzer going off or the smell of floor wax and it is 1985 all over again, when I am skinny and self-conscious. I hate my legs, my flat hair, my flat chest, my chipped front tooth. I am scared of change rooms and crowded cafeterias. I am scared of myself, of the secret heart inside me that doesn't beat like it is supposed to and makes me different. I don't know I'm queer yet, but I know what happens to kids who don't fit in.

Every time I walk through the front doors of another high school, I remember what it was like to hide, to pretend, to practise not being different. I watch the kids, noticing the ones who avoid my eyes instead of staring. I am not here to change the minds of the many. I am here for the kids who think they are alone. The skinny boy with the long eyelashes who knew he was a fag even before they started calling him one in gym class. The Catholic girl who confesses only to her journal and prays that God will make it go away. The oldest daughter of a former beauty queen whose mother makes her see a shrink once a week ever since she got busted French kissing a girl named Marie on the couch in the rec room when they were supposed to be working on a three-dimensional model of a molecule. These are the kids I want to be seen by, the kids I want to stand in front of, unashamed and unafraid. I don't say I'm queer, because I don't need to. I wear cowboy shirts and big black boots and tell stories. I tell them that my writing pays all my bills, that I love my job, that they can be artists too, not just lawyers and dentists and assistant managers.

A couple of months ago, I got an email from an English teacher asking me to come and perform in a high school in Surrey, the conservative town situated southeast of Vancouver. Surrey, with a school board prone to banning books with titles like *Heather Has Two Mommies*. Did I want to risk a gig in Surrey? Absolutely not. I was halfway through writing a polite letter saying that I was busy that day, when I stopped to consider what school must be like there for young homos. How could I turn my back on the queer kids who needed me most? How often was a gay storyteller even allowed inside a high school in Surrey? I said yes, and immediately started to stress out about it. I arranged to bring my friend the punk-rock cello player with me, for moral and musical support.

A couple of weeks before the gig, I got another email from the English teacher. He explained that one of the other teachers had done some research on me and had raised concerns about "inappropriate sexual content" in my work, and would I mind sending copies of all the stories I was planning to read so that the staff could make sure I wouldn't say anything that might offend anyone? There would be a couple of Mormon kids in the audience, he added, and the school wanted to avoid any trouble.

I took a deep breath, smoked two cigarettes, and called him on the phone. I liked him, and I knew he meant well. I told him that the reason I do gigs in high schools is to show the kids that being an artist is a viable career option, to inspire them to believe that writing or painting or playing an instrument is just as important as algebra or volleyball. I told him that I would never do or say anything that would jeopardize the chance to bring other artists into his school, and that I was there to encourage creativity, not homosexuality. I told him that I wouldn't say anything too gay, but that I looked queer and if looking queer was also against school rules then I could recommend another talented storyteller who also might offend the Mormon kids because he is from the Dogrib First Nation and believes in magic and different gods, but at least he was heterosexual.

So the cello player and I did two one-hour sets in a Surrey school last week. I told wholesome stories, and she swore once in one of her songs, but none of the teachers batted an eye, they were so relieved that we didn't bring up how obviously queer we both were. The principal gave us each a mug and a matching pen, and a thank-you card with a cheque inside.

That night we both received MySpace messages from the girl with the purple brush-cut who sat in the front row during the afternoon set. She was smiling in her picture, her cheek pressed up against her girlfriend, who had orange hair and a nose ring. She was just writing to tell us how much she loved our show; that it was the best thing her school had ever seen. I clicked on her profile. It said she was sixteen, a lesbian, and an aspiring writer.

Many Little Miracles

It is a bit of a miracle that I was there at all. It was an accident that almost didn't happen, a detour that I didn't mean to take. I was there only because I said yes, I would love to come and tell stories in a small town in northern Ontario. What I meant to say was no, I do not want to take a five-hour flight followed by a six-hour bus ride to do a one-hour gig. But I have never excelled at the fine art of saying no, so instead I asked for too much money and hoped someone in Ontario would just say no for me. My bluff was called, and I was forced to say yes, because of the money. Yes, I would be happy to go to Port Elgin, Ontario, and entertain 200 gay, lesbian, bisexual, and transgendered members of the Canadian Auto Workers Union during their annual "Pride in the Workplace" conference. I would fly home from Calgary on a Thursday afternoon and take a plane to Toronto first thing Friday morning. Port Elgin was too far, and I was tired of the road.

I should have stayed home and mowed the lawn. I had a week's worth of emails to answer, and a garden full of weeds to pull. I missed my dogs. I almost didn't go. If I were even marginally better at saying no, I would have missed the whole thing. If I had been invited by a group of overzealous academics from the women's studies department, or a subversive high school drama teacher, or even an earnest collective of liberal librarians, I would have stayed home, done my laundry, and made a giant pot of chili.

But I was curious. I had never met a queer auto worker before. Fags who built Fords. Transsexuals who assembled transmissions. Were they built tougher than big-city gay waiters were? Were they harder than hairdressers, more calloused than a carpenter dyke's hammer hand? Could they get me a discount on a Ford Focus station wagon? Did they get a union job on the assembly line right out of high school just like their dad and older brother did? Did they dream of this job, or did they drop out of college and into dark blue coveralls? Did they ever lay awake in bed at night and wonder how many more brand new Trans Ams the future world will actually need, or did they sometimes wish they owned a Toyota or one of those hybrid things the yuppies like to feel good about driving, not for looks or reliability, but because of the price of gas these days?

The LGBT members of the CAW were there to organize, to strategize and fight for the right to work alongside their straight union brothers and sisters without fear or harassment. Together they imagined a workplace where they didn't have to lie or leave out parts of their lives when the guy who worked beside them asked what they got up to over the long weekend. They dreamed of a day when the truth didn't cost them a promotion, a day when they could walk all the way across the parking lot alone without needing to look over their shoulder to see if anyone was following too close behind, even after a graveyard shift.

They were there to fight for all of these things, and I was there to entertain them. I wore my steelworkers T-shirt to show some solidarity, but one of the organizers took me aside and told me to change because auto workers and steel-workers had been in a longstanding feud over fundamental beliefs that were too complicated to get into, and it was a sore spot that I would be better off not bringing attention to.

I made a muscle-bound leather daddy who was the shop steward in a muffler factory cry like a baby when I told the one about my nephew the crossdresser. I sold a book to a man who leaned across the table to tell me in a low whisper that he couldn't read, and that his boyfriend had promised to read my stories aloud to him in bed before they fell asleep at night.

Later, in the bar, I met a sixty-year-old woman who had worked on an assembly line since just after her sixteenth birthday, and had been forced into early retirement by a twenty-eight-year old manager with a Master's degree in squeezing blood from stones. When I asked her what she was going to do next, she pretended she hadn't heard my question, then whipped out her gold Visa card and ordered another round of tequila shooters for everyone at the table.

There was a painfully shy transwoman sitting quietly alone in the corner of the bar, her shoulders slumped for-ward in an attempt to shrink some of her six-foot frame into the smaller body it looked to me like she wished she lived inside of instead. She mouthed the words to the tinny karaoke songs, and sipped ginger ale through a thin pink straw. The leather daddy finished off his beer and strutted across the room and asked her to dance with him. When she looked up at him, I saw the lines that framed her lipsticked mouth stretch into a beautiful grin that revealed a face that seemed suddenly thirty years younger, when her life was simpler and less lonely.

"How could I say no to you?" she purred, and covered her mouth with one palm.

I watched the two of them slow dance to "Stand By Your Man" by Tammy Wynette, and it was such a beautiful sight, him in his GWGs and her with a run up the back of one leg of her nylons, that I had to just thank providence that somehow I ended up being there to see it.

Ramble On

I love how once you hit Lillooet, 250 kilometres northeast of Vancouver, the big-city dank disappears into thin dry air somewhere halfway around a corner into the past in your rearview mirror and all of a sudden the smell of sage and tinder dry desert tells your nostrils you have officially left the city.

I love the muted sand and burnt bark brown of the ponderosa pines and the cerulean shine of a sun that will burn the mercury into the thirties later in the day. But right now it's dawn and the dew still shines cold and silver in shiny beads on the hood of my brand new Ford Ranger Supercab pickup truck with suicide doors and Sirius satellite radio. The only thing that could make this day any sweeter would be a little sixteen-foot travel trailer to tow behind, which I also bought last week, full of mismatched seventies dishes and the smell of bacon cooking. I immediately mounted two sparkling new propane tanks like fresh dentures on the front hitch, put on a pair of brand new biased ply tires, and hit the road Monday afternoon, sixteen hours after I had wrapped up my last gig for a month and mere minutes after the mechanic on the corner finished re-packing the wheel bearings on my trailer with fresh clean road grease and my laundry was close enough to being dry.

This has been a dream of mine since I was eleven and my Great Uncle Jack, my dad's mom's favourite of her three brothers, took me and my husky BuckBuck camping at the warm springs outside of Atlin, BC, for a week. Those seven days smack in the sunburnt stretch of late summer in 1980 are etched epic into my childhood mythology: for once I was the only kid, which felt light years away from my usual reality, where I was the eldest of over twenty cousins and the chronic babysitter and default fall guy. I was always the one who should have known better and/or been setting a proper example whenever one of my many charges came back to the house bleeding or busted for shoplifting Jelly Tots or Lick-Em Stix from the corner store.

My Uncle Jack's birthday was August the twenty-third, and mine was the eleventh. We cooked pork chops and Minute Rice and canned cream corn every night, plus bacon and eggs of course for breakfast and either Lipton Chicken Noodle soup in a box or Zoodles and white bread toast for lunch, depending on what we felt like, since it was our birthday month and who would be any the wiser since it was just the two of us. We never made broccoli or anything like that because my mom wasn't around to tell me to eat something green and his mom, my great grandma Monica, who was never a big fan of vegetables herself, died three years earlier at the ripe old age of 100 and who knows, maybe that's where we both got our broccoli aversion from, but it didn't seem to have done Great Grandma Monica any harm, so what the hell. Besides, skipping the greenery just leaves room in your stomach for another pork chop, or so went our logic.

I slept in my very own pup tent and at night I could hear wild horses grazing in the meadow all around me and I was scared for sure, but never enough that I had to wimp out and go sleep in the trailer like my little sister Carrie would have done if she wasn't back home in Whitehorse going to Boys and Girls Club all week long to play badminton and make stupid stuff out of popsicle sticks and pipe cleaners because my mom couldn't take her to the office anymore since her promotion, and unlike myself, Carrie tended to get bored hanging around my dad's shop and was always under his feet whenever he turned around, whining that there was nothing to do.

I spent all week catch-and-releasing frogs and tadpoles, reading Hardy Boys novels from the nickel bin at the Sally Ann, and perfecting the finishing work on my tree fort, which was cleverly camouflaged in the willows on the other side of the warm springs so I wouldn't have to share it with any of the American tourists' kids who came and went every couple of nights or so.

But what I remember most about that camping trip was that Uncle Jack let me go shirtless all day every day, saying that there was no difference between my chest and that of a little boy's, at least for another couple of years or so, not to mention it was hot, and since when had they passed the stupid law that said little girls had to wear shirts while swimming in the back country anyway?

So I slipped through a week of summer bare-chested, sunburnt, blissed out, and feeling blessed, and I have wanted a truck and trailer of my very own ever since. Mine is a '71 Skylark, tan and white with a brown and orange interior and harvest gold appliances. For some reason, it reminds me of growing up in the seventies. Something about the smell, I think, or maybe it's the beanbag ashtray. It feels like freedom, like I can go anywhere and still be at home. Like I own the roof over my head: it's not rented from someone else, and best of all, it moves. If my neighbours aren't friendly, I can pull out and go find a friendlier place to mooch free wireless from. I can eat pork chops every night for a week if I feel like it. I can go topless. I can smoke in my sleeping bag and burn candles almost too close to the curtains and leave the dishes if I want and listen to *Led Zeppelin II* over and over again and no one will complain or change it to The Cowboy Junkies. I can go for days without wasting valuable stomach space digesting anything green. Hey, Uncle Jack lived like this for years, and it didn't hurt him any. Besides, I always wanted to be just like him when I got old enough to not have to ever grow up.

Dirty Rotten Cock Knockers

If you travel far and/or frequently enough for long periods of time, eventually you will begin to see a pattern. I'm speaking loosely here, of course. There are never any fixed rules in the downtown core of our little global village; I cannot guarantee you that it is impossible to find a proper cup of tea south of the 49th parallel, but I can safely say it is improbable, unless you are in Massachusetts or some such state where your odds might improve to unlikely. One should generally avoid making sweeping generalizations about places you have only ever passed through, but I can tell you that it seems to me that you can stay up all night by accident in New York City, but in Ottawa they wrap up all the fun by the stroke of midnight. It's easy to score some sticky bud in San Francisco or Seattle, but don't drink the tap water. The weed is weak and tastes leafy and is hard to come by in the UK, where booze is the intoxicant of choice, and it's cheaper than drinking their flat ginger ale. In America, the customer is always right, but in Amsterdam the customer is almost never right (especially if they think you are American), except for those rare occasions where the customer may have had a point or two but who was listening, and besides, can't you see I'm on the phone here? I usually appreciate this more hands-off Dutch approach to customer service until I experienced an unfortunate series of events in the red-light district just last week, on my second trip to my most beloved haven, this pothead pervert's hedonistic heaven.

My lovely lanky lady friend and I were in a women-
owned and operated high-end latex and rubber fetish wear
store just moments after having both simultaneously fallen
in love with the ridiculously long-lashed and beautiful man-
boy who worked in the mushroom and herbal ecstasy shop
right next door. Like I said, I love Amsterdam. I was trying
to talk her into trying on this red and white latex nursey
outfit we both knew she would never buy, and cajoling her
into buying a butt plug we both knew was one sphincter size
out of her comfort zone. She insisted through the change
room curtain that the black latex corset I had just laced up
for her was far more practical and versatile, and the butt
plug was just insensitive. When I stepped aside to let another immaculately dressed Dutch shopper squeeze past
me in the narrow aisle between racks of rubber uniforms
and rows of gas masks, my shoulder bag brushed the corner
of a six-foot glass display shelf. The lightning-like crash of
glass was followed by a brutal downpour of butt plugs and a
flash flood of nipple clips and feather ticklers. When it was
all over, I had a shard of something sharp embedded in the
back of my left hand, and there were two broken cocks that
someone was going to have to answer for. Expensive ones.
Big heavy cocks carved by hand out of granite, with razor
sharp edges. The last thing a world traveller would want,
and the shopkeeper seemed to think I owed her 180 Euros,
which is about 250 smackeroos back home. I argued that
not only was it not prudent for a retailer to display giant
stone penises atop shaky shelving units alongside a skinny
public thoroughfare, but that the identical shelf still stand-

ing intact next to the one I had demolished was also an accident waiting to happen, and that it was lucky for all of us that there wasn't a small child with a soft skull nearby when it all came down who might have been brained by a phallus of such weight and density, and that I felt it was the store's responsibility to ensure that the cocks were all displayed in a safe and secure fashion, especially the more dangerous ones. It was a miracle none of us had lost a toe, I said, eyeing my lady friend, who was ever so slowly sidling closer to the front door.

The salesgirl insisted that I was going to have to cough up the cash for the damages, and dialed up her boss on the cordless phone, her lips pursed tight from all the trouble I was causing her. Meanwhile, the other shopper, who in my mind had a hand in the mishap herself, huffed and narrowed her eyes at me and agreed with the clerk, and went on at some length about personal responsibility, a public-stoning tone in her almost accentless English. The store owner then lectured me about how in Holland it is not the retailer who bears the burden of liability insurance, but the individual, and that if she were to go over to her friend's house and burn a hole in the leather couch with a cigarette, her own insurance, not the homeowner's, would cover it, that Holland was a You Break, You Buy country, all the way.

I informed her that there was no such thing as cock-knocking insurance where I came from, and that I would have happily paid for both giant granite cocks without ar-gument if I had picked them up, which I would never do in the first place, and broken them through any fault of my own, which is unlikely, in Canada or Amsterdam, because it was the right thing to do, but that I flat out refused to pay for hazardous heavy cocks that rained down on innocent consumers from atop substandard shelving that was going to get her nothing but sued one day if it wasn't fixed. I told her to call the police, and we would let them inspect the remaining shelf and decide who should pay the piper for the penises in question.

That's right about when she started screaming about how she had a headache and didn't need my litigious American bullshit attitude and how in her country people pay for what they break, when I caught a blue streak of denim flash past me as my friend dashed for the door. For some reason, I interrupted the raging retailer to repeat that actually I was Canadian, and then I passed the handset back to the sales-girl and bolted into the street after her. The salesgirl chased us halfheartedly for a block before turning back to tend to her abandoned fetish wear. We sprinted past window after window of bored ladies of the late afternoon smoking and talking on their cellphones under red neon tubes and into a coffeeshop, breathing in heaving lungfuls of hash smoke and laughing. Too bad we couldn't go back and visit our boyfriend the mushroom salesman. The price you pay for being on the lam in Amsterdam.

Later, in the hotel room, we called each other Bonnie and Clyde, and it was hot.

Pass the Time

I'm not going to torture my reflection in the mirror looking for reasons, nor am I about to torment myself with annoying existential questions seeking answers. I'm just going to accept it. I pass a lot more these days, and I'm not sure exactly why that is.

Some would say this means I am accessing male privilege, that folks like me who are regularly read as men are often treated with more respect and taken more seriously, especially by other men, and that the streets are safer for us than they are for our often more feminine companions, and of course they would be partly right. But, as any tranny worth hir salt will surely tell you, passing as male among men is for the most part a tenuous and dangerous space to inhabit, and reality is rarely so black and white. Sometimes I really like passing as a boy or young man, especially when I find myself in the company of winking dirty old men who see a little of the boy they used to be in the strapping young fella they think I am. I'll admit it, it's fun sometimes, not to mention educational. But then there are other times when passing can be hazardous to your health, like last August at a truck stop bathroom just off the highway somewhere in Saskatchewan. That trucker was more than convinced I was a smooth-shaven young tourist lad, and that he wanted to show me the full-sized sleeper he had on the brand new big rig that he had parked so proudly behind the restaurant. He was horny and aggressive and I had to be rescued by my lady friend. Then there are times when it just gets weird and complicated, like it did last week with my new landlord.

I have spent a good part of the last thirty-eight years perfecting my method of coping with the gender confusion of strangers, and I have developed my own set of guidelines in terms of my own reaction to the often unpredictable behaviour of an individual experiencing a bout of dysphoria or panic upon meeting me for the first time. My first rule is not to say or do anything too gender-specific, and to just let the stranger in question continue believing I am whatever gender they assume me to be, the catch being, of course, that I am quite often not certain just which gender box I should continue to help them make me fit into. This can get tricky quickly.

I recently relocated to Ontario for eight months, to be the writer-in-residence at Carleton University. After briefly perusing the rental listings in Ottawa, I decided to rent me and the dogs a little house in the country. I found a one-bedroom cottage on the water about half an hour west of the city and tracked down the landlord. Within a minute of meeting him, it became apparent that he thought I was a young lad, as they say in the valley. I weighed my options, after silently calculating the odds that he would prefer renting the cute little house he wanted to retire to one day to a young lad, regardless of how clean-cut I might appear, to how he might feel about turning the keys over to a big old dyke, no matter how gainfully employed I might be, if only for the next eight months. I took into consideration all the facts I had at hand: the guy appeared to be in his fifties, and this was a town of 600 people. I opted for letting him continue to think I was a young lad, and allayed any fears he might have about my irresponsible youth costing him any money by paying him four months' rent up front in cash. When he asked me for the third time just what it was I did for a living again, and looked increasingly skeptical when I repeated that I was the author of five books, I finally gave him one of my new CDs just to prove to him that I was telling the truth. I really was a storyteller.

Ironic, I know.

A couple of nights after I moved in, the landlord dropped by with his wife. He was almost overly impressed with the new paint job in the living room, but seemed vaguely nervous about something, or maybe he was just in a hurry to get home. But he was definitely acting a little weird; it was kind of hard to pin down. I noticed he smirked knowingly and winked at his wife when he thought I wasn't looking when I told him how the kitchen was going to be sort of a pale gold colour, and the bedroom a rather complimentary shade of deep pumpkin.

We had moved on to discussing the water pump in the basement and getting the well water tested when he blurted out what he had obviously been building up to bringing up since he had walked through the door.

"I listened to your CD. You didn't tell me you were gay. Not that I would care. That's your business. It's all good with me. I don't care who you sleep with, or what colour you paint the hallway." He smiled nervously, and swallowed hard.

"Thanks, Scott. Right back at you," I told him.

This made him laugh, as his wife shifted uncomfortably from her perch on the basement stairs. Scott continued, desperate to prove to me he was down with renting to a homosexual. "I don't even mind if you have your boyfriend over or whatever, as long as you pay the rent."

This, of course, was when it all became hilariously clear to me. Not only was I passing, I was passing as a gay man. My new landlord had done some soul searching and had found it in his heart to warmly embrace my lifestyle, and trust my superior decorating skills.

There are now three gays in this village. When I told Patrick, one-half of the only gay couple in town, about my dilemma, he crossed both arms and pursed his lips. "Well, you'll have to clear that up right away." He was only half-kidding. "This is a small town. There's only room for one queen, and I was here first. And don't you forget it, sister."

Window Seat

She was sitting in my window seat. I mean, really sitting. Shoes off, painted toenails tucked sideways under her bum, reading a magazine. She looked real comfortable; the slender index finger on her right hand twirling around an errant lock of professionally bleached bangs before tucking it back behind a delicate ear. She was beautiful, but I was tired. I can only sleep on an airplane if I get a window seat, and she had parked her pretty little ass in mine.

When I pointed this out politely but firmly, she blinked several times at me, her eyes round and blue, her mascara job immaculate, and informed me that it was okay with her if I just took her aisle seat, since she was already all settled in, as was the nice lady next to her.

She was cute, and I almost fell for it. I was recently single, freshly tattooed, and on my way to New York City. She had a very fetching way of raising just one eyebrow in a manicured question mark, and I have always been vulnerable to the persuasive skills of certain kinds of ladies. She was smart enough to know an easy mark with a window seat when she saw one, and I came this close to trading a chance to nap for the opportunity to do the gentlemanly thing in front of a hot stranger and her fifty-something seatmate.

I must be getting old, because after quickly weighing my options, I chose the nap.

"Shouldn't we at least be in our assigned seats while the plane is taking off?" I insisted kind of half-heartedly.

"You know, in case we crash, so they can find our DNA or whatever?"

The nice lady in the middle seat nodded in silent agreement, yes, indeed we should be in our proper seats for DNA identification purposes, then tucked her paperback into the seat pocket and hauled her pantsuited bum out into the aisle beside me.

Hot girl let out a disappointed sigh and leaned forward to retrieve her shoes from under the seat in front of her. That is when her designer T-shirt slid up to reveal a long stretch of her naked back, lean and heavily tattooed with leopard spots.

Just give her your goddamn window seat, for the love of Christ, she's a stone cold fox, whispered the little red devil that always wants to get laid from his perch just behind my left ear.

You need to get some bed rest so you can be sharp for your performance tonight, the librarian angel reminded me from my other shoulder. *You should be thinking of your immune system, not hot strangers with full back tattoos. These long flights, the recycled air. You just don't handle the jet lag like you used to. Take a nap. It's for the best.*

I folded up my leather jacket for a pillow and stuffed it into the drafty crack next to the plexiglass window and closed my eyes right away, hoping to nod off immediately.

But I've always been prone to eavesdropping.

Nice lady beside me was asking hot girl a lot of questions, and her answers were keeping me awake.

No, she wasn't married, and yes, she was going to New

York on business too. She had just moved to San Francisco, but she still spent a lot of time in New York for work. She was a hairdresser for a high-end salon, but no, she wasn't staying at a hotel, she was crashing at her ex-girlfriend's house, and yes, she meant girlfriend, not friend who was a girl.

I sat up straight and opened my eyes. Nice lady smacked my arm gently like nice ladies are allowed to do when teasing younger folks these days. "Oh, now he's awake. You heard that part, didn't you? Men. I read in *Cosmo* that two girls together is one of their all-time top fantasies. I asked my husband about it, but he pled the fifth on that one. How about you, sir?"

Nice lady laughed and then coughed and dug around in her bag, hauled out a roll of breath mints, offered one to each of us. Hot girl smirked and raised another eyebrow, awaiting my answer.

I felt the blood rush into my cheeks. "Two girls together? Well … I'm not going to say I don't like the thought of it."

All three of us laughed then, for three different reasons. We continued this sort of a three-legged dog of a conversation all the way from Chicago to La Guardia. The lesbian hairdresser's name was actually Darby, and Denise sold X-ray software to dental technicians. All three of us spent a lot of time on the road. When I told them I was a writer, Denise said she'd never heard of me, but that she would be sure to look me up "on the Google" when she got home. While we were waiting for our bags, Darby asked me if I wanted to hop a cab into Manhattan with her, since her company was paying for it.

When the taxi pulled up in front of my hotel, I took a deep breath, and then I took a chance.

"Want to come show me your city from the window of my hotel room?"

Darby sat back in her seat and licked the lipsticked edges of a smile. "How do you even know I'm your kind of girl?"

"I saw your luggage, remember? Two gigantic pink suit-cases, plus carry-on? For one long weekend? I can tell that you're my kind of girl."

She shook her head. "I'm almost late for dinner with the ex."

"Call her and tell her your plane was delayed. Beauty of cellphones."

She slipped me her business card, told me to call her in the morning. "Poor Denise. Wait till she Googles you tonight. Remember what she said when her husband picked her up? "A lesbian and a famous writer, Dennis. She's a hairdresser to the stars and he's on a book tour. You just never know who you're going to meet on the airplane these days."

Right-Winged

G'day. I've been living in the valley, as they say, digging my truck out of the ever-abundant snow every couple of days to foray east on Highway 417 into Ottawa for dim sum or laundry or office hours or sometimes even a plane ride. I wouldn't say I'm lonely in my little cottage on the river in the country, but I have noticed that I am even more prone to chatting up strangers than usual these days, and this poor fellow was stuck next to friendly old me for the four-hour flight home.

I try not to make assumptions about people, so I didn't jump to conclusions just because he was young, handsome, fit, wearing Italian jeans, and smelling of Guerlain cologne (I think it was Vetiver). These were all fine clues, to be sure, but I didn't become actively suspicious that my row mate was a homosexual until he asked the gentleman in the aisle seat if he would mind switching places so that his friend could come sit next to him. His "friend" turned out to be the even prettier boy waggling his slender fingers at us from a couple of rows back.

Any lingering doubts that the fellow sitting next to me was as gay as a cross-Canada flight was long dissipated immediately upon take-off. As the plane groaned against gravity and left the tarmac behind, he batted his eyelashes in a dramatic panic. Then when the plane bumped and dipped through a bit of turbulence as we rose above the cloudbank blanketing Vancouver, his hands escaped his lap altogether and fluttered around his face like two terrified humming-birds. That is when I noticed that his hands were so white and soft and nubile they looked like they would have be-longed better on a marble church statue of a cherub. His pretty boyfriend patted his lover's thigh in sympathy, and then promptly put on his complimentary headphones and dialed up some cartoons on his little TV screen.

So of course we get to talking. It is both true and some-what tragic how much of my human interactions take place in, on my way to, or waiting for an airplane as of late, but there it is; I like to meet people and find out what they are about and how life has been treating them.

This guy was a lawyer and his boyfriend was an art student studying painting, which was cool with the lawyer, who could afford to bring home the bacon for both of them if they were to need bacon, but from the looks of them, the lawyer was more likely to be bringing home the bacon-fla-voured textured vegetable protein-based meat-free substi-tute, were I to guess, which I try not to do.

I don't remember how it came up, but in addition to being a young, gay, hip, well-educated, and well-to-do ur-ban professional, all of which seemed fairly in character to me, he was also a card-carrying member of the Progressive Conservative Party of Canada, a staunch fan of none other than Prime Minister Stephen Harper himself, and a self-identified libertarian.

I had heard of such a creature and read first-hand ac-counts by others about their encounters with right-wing gays, but he was the first one I had ever actually came face to face with in the wild. I guess I have been sheltered for years by life in East Vancouver, what with the west coast being a rather hostile environment for conservatives in general, and the gay ones being especially rare, often avoiding danger by camouflaging themselves as young gay liberals.

But this guy was shameless, practically flaunting his neo-conservative plumage in broad daylight.

Now I know a lot of queers that would have just assumed they were sitting with the enemy, brushing thighs with his pink-hued designer sheep's clothing, but I was fascinated. Descending proudly from a long line of Yukon frontiersmen with heavy survivalist tendencies and plenty of cash and ammunition buried somewhere on their property as I am, I was curious as to how a velvet-palmed lawyer living in a condo boasting its own Second Cup on the ground floor could self-identify as a libertarian. This fellow was as queer as a tulip in a cornfield, and obviously didn't even shovel his own driveway, much less own a decent generator in case of natural disaster or war or the eventual collapse of our bloated and ineffective government infrastructures.

At least we could both agree on gun control, but for very different reasons. Him because he believes that all persons are the absolute controllers of their own lives and should be free to do whatever they wish with their persons or property, provided they allow others the same liberty, and that a limited government is necessary for the maximization of such liberties. And me because I travel a lot and sometimes strangers want to kill me for no other reason than that they think I am in the wrong bathroom, and the next time a redneck with a moustache chases me and my girlfriend for over an hour on a logging road in the bush just because he doesn't like the look of us, I don't want to be the only one without a firearm, just in case. Plus, next spring my neighbour Pete said he'd take me wild turkey hunting.

Of course I had to ask the obvious question. Didn't he have trouble aligning his love of Stephen Harper's politics with his own personal, I don't know, gayness? He admitted that he and old Steve didn't see eye to eye on everything, of course. But he lost me when he started in about global warming being only one theory, and I told him he needed to get his ass up north if he wanted evidence, and then all of a sudden it was time to return our tray tables and seatbacks to their upright position.

I kept his business card, just in case, though. You never know when you're going to need a corporate lawyer these days. Especially one with powerful friends.

Coffee Club

When I first rented the little yellow house on the river back in September, I thought my first winter in a small Ontario town might take some getting used to. I thought that as the nights got longer and the dark got colder and the snow got deep enough, I would miss big city life and long for urban luxuries like lattés and dim sum and gay bars and street-lights, but I don't.

My favourite thing about living in Fitzroy Harbour, Ontario, population 600, is coffee club. Coffee club meets at eight o'clock every morning seven days a week except for Sundays in the winter, when everyone sleeps in a little bit and we start at nine. Rain, snow, or shine, we cluster around a well-worn wooden table in the back room of the Harbour Store, our post office-slash-liquor-slash-video-slash-corner store. From two to eight p.m., the back room of the Harbour Store doubles as a pizza and burger place and a second home and first part-time job for the town's crop of baggy-panted bored teenagers, but in the morning, it is where we gather to drink drip coffee and tell stories.

Not everyone is there every day. Sometimes the fireman is working nights or the cattle farmer is busy with a sick calf or the retired plumber's knee is too sore to risk the icy sidewalks. The old guy with the snowplow comes late when there's a blizzard, and his wife skips Sundays to go to mass, but there is always someone around. We tell jokes and do the crossword in the *Ottawa Sun* together and talk politics.

Shooting the shit, I believe, is the technical term for what it is we do.

Membership comes with benefits, such as free turnips and septic tank advice and someone's mother's shortbread cookies and a never-ending round of talk. For any storyteller worth his or her salt, it's basically a dream come true. This morning, I dragged myself out of a January slumber to don my down parka and big black Sorel snow boots to tromp the two snow-blown blocks up the street, and as always, it was worth it. I just got back from a gig in Florida, so I had alligator sightings and a New Year's Day swim in the Atlantic Ocean to recount to everyone. There was hockey talk of course, and the morning paper to skim through and discuss. This morning's Sunshine Girl had breasts that looked bigger than her head, a ratio even the fellows agreed was disturbing. There was a tearful moment and a heartfelt round of condolences when the engineer showed up for the first time since his elderly mother passed two days after Christmas. The salesman's thirteen-year-old son moped in to stay warm until the school bus showed up, certain that his life was unbearable ever since his school's snowboarding field trip was cancelled on account of the freezing rain we got last night. Carole, his mother, kissed him goodbye in front of everyone, and then after he had left for school, she took off her toque and showed us that her hair had started to grow back in after the chemotherapy, and we all said another silent prayer in our heads for her and her family.

By nine a.m, almost everyone had left for work or headed into town to pick up groceries, except for the self-employed writer, the lady who works nights at the store, Carole who is off work at least until the next round of chemo is over, and one of the twins.

It took me awhile to be able to tell the twins apart, until someone pulled me aside and explained that one of the two big burly brothers had a goatee and the clean-shaven one was gay; that was how to keep them straight, no pun intended. So Dave, the gay twin, starts complaining about being single for way too long. Sharon, the lady who works nights at the store, listened and nodded for a bit, and then piped up that her sister, who lived just a couple of towns over, happened to be recently single too, through no fault of her own of course, and maybe she could introduce the two of them, you never know, right, maybe they would hit it off. Dave blinked a couple of times and then looked at me, and then back to Sharon.

"But I'm gay. Didn't anyone tell you by now?"

Sharon's jaw dropped, then she fumbled around with it for a split second, and picked it back up again.

"Oh Dave, I didn't know," she said, swallowing hard. "I'm so sorry."

Dave crossed his big eyebrows, looking confused.

Sharon waved both hands in front of her, a bit panicked and backpedaling. "I mean, not that I'm sorry you're gay, that is not what I meant to say, I mean … what I meant was I'm sorry I didn't know, how embarrassing, not that there is anything wrong at all with you, I mean please don't get me wrong, it is totally okay to be gay."

I tried so hard not to lose it, because she was trying

so hard not to be rude, to be nice, to say the right thing, so it seemed the least I could do was not fall off my chair laughing at her, but then Dave placed a forgiving palm on her shoulder and said, "I know there's nothing wrong with being gay, Sharon. I'm the gay one, remember?"

I nearly shot Tim Horton's brand drip coffee out both nostrils.

That's the thing about living in a small town. There is only one place to get yourself a coffee. Somehow everybody just has to get along. And this always makes for a great story.

Broccoli and Cheese Sauce

With some people you can just tell, even from a distance. Maybe it was how his shoulders slumped in a kind of tired sigh, or the slow way he put one old foot in front of the other as he walked toward us. Whatever it was, I could see it in the shape of him, even from a hundred feet away. Somehow this guy had lonely written all over him.

I was in Florida for a gig, and my friend took me on a little nature walk to see alligators, which for a Yukon kid is kind of like spotting a dinosaur, they were that foreign to my Northern eyes. We were meandering along the boardwalk that led back to where we had parked the car when my friend's dog approached the old man's aging cocker spaniel and exchanged sniffs and wags.

Dogs are good for that. They can get two strangers talking who otherwise might cross the street to avoid each other. We exchanged the usual information: what kind of dog is that, how old is he, I have an old dog myself at home, her hips are sore in the winter but not so much since the glucosamine tablets, you should try them they really work, stuff like that.

The man seemed so eager to talk that I pulled out a cigarette and rested one elbow on the hand railing, settling myself in for a bit of a chat.

"Canadian, huh? Never been, but there sure are a lot of yous living in the trailer park where I've got my rig. Me and the missus retired here from New Hampshire in 2000, we used to have a little house in Sarasota, but she passed this last February. The place was too big for just me and the old dog here, we were rattling around inside that house alone, so I sold it and bought myself a little travel trailer."

It was the first week of January, but he hadn't said that his wife passed away last year, or a year ago. He said February. I knew what that meant. He was still counting his loneliness by the month. I bet if I asked him, he could still tell me how many days it had been.

I travel a lot, and over the years I have become an expert at talking to strangers. Most of them just want to talk, mostly about nothing, the weather, their kids, their old dog's hips, how often Air Canada has lost their luggage, that kind of thing, just to pass the time.

But there was something about the watery way his eyes caught mine and held them. I just knew.

"How are you doing?" I asked him softly.

"Today we're great, aren't we, boy?" He ruffled the fur on top of the spaniel's head. "Nothing like the sun to keep the old bones happy."

He thought he was answering the question most people ask, the kind of polite question you are never supposed to answer with the actual truth. So I asked him again.

"I mean, how are you really doing? It must have been tough for you, these last couple of weeks, getting through the holidays for the first time. How are you really doing?"

His eyes opened wide, like he was seeing me standing in front of him for the first time. Then he shook his head a little, as though he couldn't quite trust his ears, making the skin of his old cheeks jiggle in disbelief. It took him a minute to compose himself. I saw his shoulders relax, and then he let out a long breath.

"To tell you the honest truth, I'm having a real hard time eating my vegetables. I make a mean fish chowder, and a pretty decent cheese and onion bread, but I'm at a loss when it comes to cooking vegetables."

It's strange, the things you miss. Me, I miss the way she used to wear her socks to bed and then pull them off with her toes. I would find them hidden in the sheets when I made the bed in the morning, crumpled into little black balls, covered in dog hair. It used to drive me nuts, but not anymore, in retrospect. Now it seems kind of adorable. I miss her dirty socks, and how she never took out the recycling. He misses the way she made him eat his vegetables.

"Can I give you a bit of advice? From a seasoned bachelor?"

"Please. Please do."

"Purple cabbage." I told him. "Purple cabbage is the very best vegetable companion a bachelor could ever have. It's cheap, and you can keep one of those suckers in the crisper for two months and still make coleslaw. Full of fiber. And cheese sauce. You'd be surprised how much broccoli you can trick yourself into eating if it's covered in cheese sauce."

He nodded, his brow knitted in concentration, like he was trying to remember what broccoli looked like.

"My wife liked cabbage a lot. Used to grate it on top of

a salad. Cheese sauce. Hmm. I'd forgotten all about a good cheese sauce."

We chatted a bit more, until he glanced at his watch and realized he was almost late for lawn bowling back at the trailer park.

"I should be off. I can't be late, or old Mrs Simpson will get her panties all up in a knot. I don't know why we have to be so punctual, we're all retired for heaven's sakes, but God help me if I show up late for lawn bowling. It really was a pleasure talking to you."

He shook my hand. His was dry and still calloused. He used to work for a living, I could tell.

"You too, sir. I mean it. It was nice to meet you. Things will get easier. You're going to be just fine, you know."

"Yes," he said, almost under his breath, bending over slow and careful to clip the leash onto his dog's collar. "I suppose I will."

You Are Here

ONE: DOWN THE TWO MILE HILL

It used to be that the only way to get to downtown White-horse from the Alaska Highway was by going down the Two Mile Hill. The story I always heard was that the Two Mile Hill is called that on account of how it's two miles long from the highway cutoff right down to Main Street, but just recently someone cornered me in the Capital Hotel at happy hour and informed me that actually, the Two Mile Hill got its name because the hill itself is only one mile long coming down, but it sure feels like two on your way back up. Who knows the real story, since the guy who told me that last bit was drunk at the time, plus almost everyone in his family is known to be playing a long game with a short hand, as my grandma would say.

However it came by its name, the Two Mile Hill wraps itself like a bent elbow around the clay cliffs that frame the west side of downtown Whitehorse; the old part with all the little wooden houses built by the soldiers in the forties so they would have a place to live when the highway was finished. The clay cliffs, well, I guess the clay cliffs are called the clay cliffs because they're made from real clay, cool and soft and grey and silky between your fingers when it rains.

A couple of years ago, someone from the government who didn't grow up here and so didn't know any better decided that the Two Mile Hill wasn't metric enough for the times, and they tried to change the name of the hill to Jack London Boulevard. They put up a new sign and everything, but only the tourists ever called it Jack London Boulevard, and nobody else knew what you were on about if you said turn down Jack London Boulevard, or I was driving up Jack London Boulevard one day, and so it never stuck. When I went home last Christmas, I noticed that they had given up on the whole Jack London Boulevard thing, and an even bigger sign had been erected that said Two Mile Hill, just so people knew to keep on calling it what they had been calling it all along.

It's stuff like this that makes my dad want to bury his cash in the ground behind his shop, just so the government won't get it and spend it on fancy signs for old roads with new names that nobody uses.

"Wonder how much that fiasco set the taxpayers back?" he said, gearing down for the curve halfway down the hill and steering with one elbow, so he could light a smoke.

It used to be that at the bottom of the hill on the left hand side of the road into town there was a marsh, all full of willow bushes that flashed the silver side of their leaves when the breeze picked up and scruffy pine and spruce trees reaching their long roots down into the permafrost for a foothold to fight the wind from. The marsh filled the space between the river that ran alongside my hometown and the road that led into it, lush and green by northern standards, full of birds and antique cans and bottles left there by the old-timers, the dreamers and the drunks that lived down by the river before the city tore their shacks down and made them pay taxes and built a proper dump to put all the empty bottles in.

I used to drive past the marsh every morning at five o'clock, on my way to work to serve breakfast to busloads of retired Americans on their way to see their forty-ninth state. I worked the five-thirty a.m. to one-thirty p.m. shift in the dining room of the Travelodge Hotel for four summers, and on weekends in the winters. Everyone still called the hotel the Travelodge, even though the new owners had bought the hotel years ago, and they renamed it the Sheffield and printed up different menus and made us wear sea-foam green uniforms instead of the usual black pants and white shirts. Then they put in a buffet breakfast table so they could feed more busloads faster, which meant less tips for us since the customers got up and filled their own plates, all we had to do was bring coffee and water and prune juice and the bill and clean up after them. Then an American chain bought the hotel and called it the Westmark, just like their other hotels all over Alaska, and we had to wear gold name tags and bring around a little tray of sour cream and chives and fake bacon bits for the baked potatoes, and say things like, "Welcome to the Westmark Whitehorse, gateway to Alaska, the last frontier. Would you care to look at our menu, or just help yourself to our breakfast buffet?"

It got so every once in a while I would leap right out of a dead sleep in a cold sweat with the smell of buttered toast and BenGay still caught up in my nostrils from the day before. I would slip out of bed and into the long blue dawn and down the highway into town. Every time I drove past the marsh I would have to slow down to thirty clicks or so, just in case a coyote or a deer darted out of the brush and into the road. One time I saw a lynx glide out of the bushes and cross both lanes in four satiny strides. I watched a blue heron gobble up a frog one morning, and the image of its impossibly long and graceful legs appeared behind my eyelids whenever I closed them, and got me through my shift that day.

A few years back, Wal-Mart talked the City of Whitehorse into paying several million taxpayer dollars to backfill the marsh with gravel so they could build a store there. Think of the jobs it will create, my aunties argued with me, think of the bargains, finally we won't have to pay whatever the shops on Main Street decide we're going to have to pay for a new pair of jeans, plus there will be a pharmacy and one of those machines you can print up your digital photos on, with the red-eye remover and the white borders and the whole nine yards, just like you see in the big malls down south. Finally, everything you can get in Vancouver or Edmonton, but without the plane ride.

Now when you drive down the Two Mile Hill and take the corner that still wraps itself around the end of the clay cliffs, you pass the Wal-Mart, two car lots, a Radio Shack, a dollar store, a family restaurant, and a drive-thru Starbucks that all squat in a neon square bordered by sidewalk where the marsh used to be. The gateway to the last frontier now looks a lot like Prince George, or Fort St. John or Thunder Bay or Red Deer. The ravens gather and gurgle around the blue dumpster behind the McDonald's. The pavement in the parking lot gets so hot in the summer that the air ripples above it, a desert of concrete sprinkled with shriveled up French fries and glinting hubcaps left behind when the RV's tires scraped up against the curb that the city workers built around the new stoplights and the traffic circle. Now we have a Boston Pizza and a brand new KFC, an A&W, a Burger King, and two Tim Horton's, one for smokers and one for those who have quit. Now Whitehorse looks like anywhere else, at least from the warm side of the windshield, just driving through. If it wasn't for the sideways sloping shadows that stretch across the chip seal under the midnight sun, if it wasn't for the wind-worn spine of the clay cliffs still sheltering the place where the marsh used to be, if it wasn't for the shape of the curves in the river that still runs past where they built the Wal-Mart, maybe I wouldn't know I was home at all.

TWO: OH, WHAT A LIFE

On February 15, 1949, Florence Daws stepped off the White Pass and Yukon Route train and down onto the frozen wooden sidewalk at the foot of Main Street in Whitehorse. She carried one suitcase and had her son David, who was almost two years old, slung on one hip. She had just turned twenty-nine, and she was three months pregnant.

Her husband Al had hitched a ride on a postal truck from Vancouver a couple of weeks before, to find them a place to rent and look for work. Al had inhaled something he shouldn't have during the war, and the doctor had told him that his damaged lungs needed a dry climate. He had heard stories about the Yukon, all full of tales of two jobs for every strong back and all the dry fresh air a fella could breathe. Al had originally dreamed of taking his family to Australia, but who could afford it?

Flo had been born in London, England, in 1919. She was working in a munitions factory at the end of the war when she met and married Al, and returned with him to Canada. She had taken the boat from Vancouver to Skagway, Alaska, and then the train to Whitehorse. She was tired, her feet hurt, and she wasn't dressed for the weather. The rest of the story goes like this, only told in a heavy Cockney accent.

Flo sat on a bench with her son in her lap and surveyed her new home. Nothing but potholes and mud roads and cold. There weren't even any street lights yet. After about an hour an American soldier pulled his truck over and rolled down his window.

"Are you lost, lady?" he asked.

"Nah," Flo says, "I'm just waitin' for me husband."

The soldier was horrified to find a pregnant woman and child left alone in the middle of February and drove straight to the police station and got them to put out an APB for one Albert Daws, ex-soldier and errant husband. They tracked him down about an hour later, drunk, at a wedding on the other side of town. The soldier helped Flo and David into his truck and they drove over to pick up the old man. He was so disgusted with my grandfather that he wouldn't even let him get up into the cab of his truck, he made him ride on the flatbed in the cold. Al directed him to a two-room wooden shack on Alexander Street, next to the clay cliffs.

"Nothing but a woodstove and a bed and an old armchair," my grandmother tells me, almost sixty years later, at her kitchen table. "Built in a little hollow too, eh?, and it rained so much that summer you 'ad to dry out the firewood before you could get it to burn. Buy your water by the bucket from the water wagon. What a life." She shakes her head and stares over my shoulder at the empty wall behind me.

Late in the summer of 1949, my mother was born. Florence Daws would go on to raise all five of her children in a series of shacks in downtown Whitehorse, not really alongside the man she married, more like in spite of him.

My grandfather passed away when I was nine, of cancer and liver troubles. He was yellow and angry and weighed less than 100 pounds when he died, and was not mourned by many. My most vivid memory of him was how he used to hang his ancient false teeth halfway out of his mouth and chase me and my sister and cousins around on the threadbare rug in the living room, until one of us whacked a toe on a doorframe or someone peed their pants or something. My gran would squawk in from the kitchen, waving her straw broom and yelling, "Knock that off, the lot of yous, or I'll belt the snot out of someone, so help me." My gran is renowned for belting the snot out of someone, baking an unsliced slab of baloney in the oven like a roast, rubbing the first ten layers of your skin off on bath night with a sandpaper-like towel straight off the clothesline, and for collecting string, tin foil, wax paper, elastic bands, and canned food. She has five children, nine grandchildren, four great-grandchildren, and two little dogs that never stop barking. She has had one of her kidneys removed, and now only drinks the green tea, to cleanse the blood. The ruptured disc in her back bothers her a lot less this winter than it did last, praise God, and she permits herself to enjoy eight Player's Light Regulars per day. Flo is eighty-nine years old and now stands only four-and-a-half feet tall. She can knit faster than anyone I've ever seen, without even looking down at her hands.

Patricia Cumming, my dad's mom, was born in Saskatoon in 1920, the daughter of Irish immigrants. She married below her, somehow, to a charming Scottish boy-soldier from Nova Scotia whose name was Don. Depending on whom you ask, my grandfather was either a dreamer or a deadbeat. Maybe he was forever chasing the next best economic opportunity, or maybe he just couldn't hold down a job, but regardless, he moved his wife and four young sons around a lot. From the prairies to the coast, and then to the bush, from Swift River to Cassiar to Carmacks, and finally to Whitehorse, where he landed a job with the highways department. The Alaska Highway is 1,523 miles of road built in a little over eight months through unforgiving country on frozen ground that never really wanted it there in the first place; so getting yourself a job repairing that highway was then and still is considered pretty steady work.

So Patricia and the boys grew up and grew Yukon roots, got Yukon jobs, and the boys went out and got Yukon girls pregnant, but not my grandfather. Patricia hoped that maybe things would be different when she followed her husband to New Zealand, that he would finally be happy there, with the sun on his back and sand from the southern hemisphere between his toes.

She finally left him in 1967 and flew back to Canada alone. She tells me the story of how she pulled the car over to the side of the road just outside of Vancouver and stared at all those road signs for a long minute.

"I figured I had two options. I could go back to Saskatoon, back to my mother, or I could go home. Home to the Yukon, where I had friends. People I loved. People who loved me back."

But she rolled the car three times just outside of Watson Lake, and totalled it. The guy who drove the mail truck gave her a lift into town after he figured out she was a local, and one of the girls who worked in the hotel tossed her the keys to her cabin down by the lake and told her to go, go make herself at home. When she filed a report with the Watson Lake police, it was discovered that she didn't even have a valid driver's licence.

"They didn't give me a hard time about it, they just drove me to the nurses' station to get checked out, and then put me on the bus to Whitehorse," she tells me. "Because I was one of them. And that was when I knew for sure that I was back in the Yukon again."

My grandma Pat still keeps her divorce papers in an old makeup case in her basement, along with letters and keepsakes from the lovers who came after. Big Pat is famous for her book collection, her eloquent and biting letters to the editor sent to an impressive list of publications, and for reading at least three newspapers front to back every day. She has four sons, eleven grandchildren, and by my last count, thirteen great-grandchildren. She has had both of her knees refitted with plastic cartilage and takes pills for the high blood pressure. She just turned eighty-eight years old in February, but she never let any of us call her Grandma until well after her seventieth birthday. Said she didn't want to feel old until she actually was.

I am a proud third-generation Yukoner, and I have always felt blessed that my family's blood somehow pooled and settled in the top left corner of the map of Canada. Being from the Yukon means you are tough, that you can light a fire and change a tire, that you aren't afraid of long nights and long winters, long highways, and long distance telephone bills. You never hear someone brag in quite the same way about being from someplace just outside of Toronto, or say that they read about Regina in a book once when they were a kid and just had to see it for themselves. But the Yukon is different, a place never meant for the weak or the spoiled. Yukon history abounds with the tales of restless or enlisted or gold-hungry men who went north to seek their fortune, but in my family it is the wives of the wanderers who settled and built and gave birth here. He might have dreamt of this place first, or most, but in the end, it was she who stayed, to write the story.

THREE: WEATHER, OR NOT.

I was born in Whitehorse General Hospital at 4:45 in the morning on August 11, 1969. It was a Sunday. My dad likes to tell the story of that morning, how he drove my mom to the hospital in the old Chevy, and how my mom sucked her breath in through her teeth and white-knuckled the hand grip above the passenger window all the way down the Two Mile Hill, on account of how the truck slid sideways around the corner because of a freak August snowstorm and hailstones the size of nickels and dimes drumming down on the windshield faster than the wipers could sweep the slush out of the way.

He claims he doesn't remember too much else about that day, except that I was born with the right number of fingers and toes, and then there was the hail, and the snow.

"In the middle of August, right? Your mom is in labour, and of course I had the wrong tires on the truck for it, and we almost hit the ditch going round the corner halfway down the hill."

"Did you wait out in the hall while Mom was in labour?"

"Course I waited out in the hall. We were still allowed to back then. Why would I want to watch something like that?"

Obviously the rest of the story came by way of my mother. She claims to remember the hailstorm, but isn't sure if it happened on the actual day I was born or not. When I pressed her for the details, she wrapped up the conversation by informing me that perhaps once I had given birth, I wouldn't need to ask why she maybe had other things on her mind at the time.

I had no evidence, and would have to rely on my father's version of the story and blurry bits of memories culled from kitchen table conversations between my uncles, who all readily confessed that it was all just a little hazy to them now, the whole second half of that decade being kind of long on feelings and short on facts like it was, the details were kind of hard to come by.

"It might have snowed that day, who knows?" My Uncle John blew a thin stream of smoke out one corner of his mouth and then smiled from under his moustache at me. "It was four in the morning. It was summer, 1969. If I was awake at that hour, then chances are I was ripped off my head and thought I was hallucinating. Who ever heard of hail in August? And since when did you start listening to my brother, anyhow? Do me a favour and see if there's any more beers in the boot room, will ya? They stay not quite frozen out there, as long as no one leaves the back door open."

The only thing better than a back porch cold beer is a snow-bank cold beer, like you find at a good old Yukon bush party at thirty below. Burning cold, we used to call it. Down south, they call it "a dry cold." Up north we just call it the weather. We also refer to anywhere that is not the Yukon as "outside," as in: "I had to send outside to get the part and it cost me a mint," or, "You know how she's from outside, and always was a little high and mighty about it too, if you ask me, and she never did learn to tolerate the cold."

"Thirty below is thirty below," my dad would always say, "and thirty below doesn't discriminate. Thirty below doesn't care how cool you think you are. Put a scarf on."

I would nod and wrap my scarf around my neck and head before I pulled the hood of my parka up, leaving just a sliver of skin around my eyes exposed, a narrow window in the wool just wide enough to see through. By the time I reached the bus stop, my breath would be frozen into beads on my eyelashes, and when I blinked they would melt against my cheeks and roll in cold tears down my face.

My Uncle John is a carpenter, and years ago I learned from him that the reason the city passed a bylaw making it illegal to construct any building taller than three stories high was not to preserve the small-town esthetic of our humble skyline; it was because of the burning cold under our feet. Whitehorse has no skyscrapers on account of the permafrost, because the ground is too frozen year-round to dig a foundation deep enough to support the weight of anything taller. It explains the absence of any underground parking in this town, too, he told me.

I always liked the thought that nature dictated the building codes of the north, not mere humans, and that my town looked the way it did because the dirt it was built on contained water that might have become ice thousands of years ago.

I found a map of Canada that the government put out that shows the different permafrost regions of the country, all colour-coded. The Yukon was mostly painted purple, meaning much of it is what they call a continuous perma-frost zone.

I took this fascinating find up to the cash register to pay for it. The cashier snapped her gum and surveyed my purchase.

"Permafrost map of Canada, huh? How interesting."

I was thrilled to have another permafrost enthusiast to converse with. "Totally. Did you know that if you build a heated structure on ground that has permafrost beneath it, you risk thawing the soil to the degree that the water will drain away and the earth will shift enough to swallow your buildin,g or snap its foundation in two?"

She looked right at me and said nothing. I assumed it was because she was hanging from my every word, so I continued.

"For instance, are you aware that the ground this store is built on is actually moving all the time, due to fluctuations in the ground's surface temperature caused by a combination of co-factors including seasonal temperature cycles, snow-pack conditions, altitude, latitude, geology, soil texture, and vegetative ground cover, not to mention the geothermal properties of the earth itself? Isn't that amazing?"

She stared over my shoulder and straight into the beige paint of the wall behind me.

"I was just joking when I said this map was interesting," she said. "You know, making small talk? As in, customer service or whatever? I couldn't actually care less about permafrost, I was just being polite."

I stepped back from her counter without meaning to. "You aren't from here then? You grow up outside somewhere?"

She shook her head like a wet husky. "I was born and raised. My mom, too. My grandfather worked on the highway. But me, I can't wait to get some place where the dirt actually thaws out in the summer, some place where you can grow more stuff than just pine trees and cranberries. I'm moving to Grande Prairie to go to dog grooming school next September. Eight more months and I'm so outta here, it's not even funny."

"Most of Alberta only has a mean annual ground temperature of plus five degrees Celsius," I told her, "resulting in sporadic discontinuous or isolated patches of permafrost at best."

"Like I said, I can hardly wait. You going to pay for this, or what?"

I wanted to tell her that without the burning cold beneath our feet, this town might have been built to look just like Grande Prairie did, and that both of our grandfathers had helped build the only road into this place, the same road the permafrost still puckers and pitches every freeze and thaw. I wanted her to know that not one single day has passed since then without construction still happening somewhere along the Alaska Highway, that it was a road that would never really be finished because of the ice that breathed beneath it, and didn't it make you think, but there was a line-up growing behind me.

In the library, I learned that you could prevent the

ground under your foundation from thawing and swallowing or heaving up your house by putting no less than two feet of dry gravel down to build upon. I learned that after the first round of buildings erected in town started sagging and moaning and leaning against each other, the government was forced to amend the building codes to account for the permafrost. I learned that the ideal northern dwelling was a small shack built up on skids to insulate the ice beneath it from the fire inside.

Then I had a thought that caused a ball of burning cold to begin to grow in my belly. What would happen if the permafrost all melts? The Wal-Mart was bad enough. What would stop them from building twelve-storey condominium towers right downtown with a comfortable view of the river?

I guess they called it permafrost back then because they thought it was going to stay frozen forever.

FOUR: SOMETHING ABOUT THE LIGHT

A few years ago, I was working on a film set, doing props on a mind-numbingly shallow and poorly written made-for-TV movie. The overtime was draining away my sense of humour while simultaneously filling up my bank account, and to pass the time I was yakking to the director of photography about adapting one of my stories into a short film. He reckoned that we could shoot the whole thing in a couple of days, maybe up in Squamish or out in Mission, someplace like that.

I shook my head and explained to him that the story takes place in the Yukon in early July, when the midnight sun barely brushes the horizon before it starts back up again, and that there was no way to replicate the kind of not quite sun that shines at three a.m. in the middle of a northern summer. It's all about the light, I told him, and the never getting dark bit was the crucial key to my main characters motivation, as the relentless light has been known to do crazy things to the minds of folks who need the night to sleep, or mark the passing of another day.

"We'd need to shoot it up north, it's the only way," I told him.

He shook his head like I had let him down somehow.

"Now what kind of an attitude is that to have? Of course I can light for the midnight sun. I can make anywhere look like anywhere, with the right gels and a light meter. That's why they call it movie magic; surely I don't need to tell you, of all people. I can't believe I get this kind of line from the props guy who found us pumpkins in July."

He was referring to the time we had to shoot a Halloween scene just before the Canada Day long weekend, the first week in July. It is a well known fact that you can't buy a pumpkin anywhere until at least the end of September at the earliest, even in the big city.

"I didn't bring you pumpkins in July, Gregory. I hand-painted fifty fucking watermelons orange, and it was a nightmare. There is no such thing as pumpkins in July."

"My point exactly," he said, "but the viewing audience never found that out. Paint a watermelon orange and voilà, you got your Halloween. Same thing goes with your midnight light."

"Those watermelons never looked at all like pumpkins, dude, and you know it. They were totally the wrong shape. In fact, I should have been fired for incompetence. They always just looked like fruit dressed up like a vegetable. An orange melon does not a squash make, my friend. And the only place that looks like the Yukon is the Yukon. That's why the city hippies flock up there in packs every spring, and risk the frostbite. There's just something about the light. You'd know it if you saw it."

There is just something about the light.

One time I left Vancouver on June 21 and floored it, heading due north. I hit the town of Williams Lake just as the sun was starting to droop in the sky a little, and I didn't stop for dinner. It was summer solstice, so the farther and faster I drove away from the equator, the longer the day became. Round about the time the porch lights were going on in Williams Lake behind me, I was already gassing up in Prince George, 240 clicks farther north. The sun was just starting to turn the smoke from the pulp mill pink there, but it wouldn't be fully dark in Prince George until I was already halfway to Dawson Creek, where the day was just starting to wind itself down. I drove for a total of four or five hours inside this perpetual sunset, feeling my wheels turning over the horizon again and again to find just a little more daylight stretched out in front of my windshield, and seeing a little more blue night creeping into my rearview mirror with every mile I left behind.

When I got to Whitehorse, my dad told me the truckers call a long haul north like that chasing the light.

My last trip home, I realized that even Wal-Mart and permafrost-proof skyscrapers and global warming will never make the sun go down any earlier in the month of June in my hometown, and that thirty below is still thirty below, no matter how close you get to park your truck to the front door of the mall. A three-in-the-morning sun will still cast sideways shadows every summer, and the slow curve of the clay cliffs will always cut the cold wind in half as soon as you round the corner halfway down the road we never stopped calling the Two Mile Hill.

There are some places that are difficult to pave over, places that will never thaw out and become soft, and there are people who still hold pictures in their head of what was torn down to make room for what now stands in its place. There are folks who remember that the Westmark used to be called the Travelodge before the guys who renamed it

the Sheffield sold it off to the Americans, but they are becoming an increasingly rare breed. There are 30,700 souls
who reside in the Yukon, but only 1,200 of them are over
the age of sixty-five. The old-timers are retiring to tell their
stories to strangers in Florida, or to their new neighbours in
a two-bedroom split level condo in Kelowna, where the fruit
trees grow and the old bones don't feel as cold.

But both of my grandmothers claim that they wouldn't
want to live anywhere else, that they can't imagine any better dirt to be buried in than the stuff that is already under
their feet. There are too many memories here to move them
all to somewhere new. This is the place they raised their
children and outlived their husbands. They tell me that almost everything about this place has changed at least once
already in their half a century here. They tell me that their
memories cannot be renovated, just forgotten. Grandma
Flo says she is blessed because all of her children turned
out happy and her eldest son is a man of God, and that if
the spot on her head turns out to be cancer, well, then, she's
lived a long and lucky life. Grandma Pat tells me that ever
since her last brother, Bob, passed away two summers ago,
she is the sole remaining of her parents' five children. She
tells me the only reason she is telling me any of this at all
is because all of her old memories become just a little bit
closer to immortal every time there is someone listening.

ACKNOWLEDGMENTS

I want to thank Mette Bach, who, during the four years these stories and columns were written and collected, was my new crush, my sweetheart, my partner, my live-in lover, my fiancée, my ex, and now one of my dearest friends. I hope I can be as remarkable a friend to her as she has been to me.

I must also thank the English Department at Carleton University, most notably the dogged and determined Jodie Medd, whose hard work and support brought me to Ottawa and made my stay as writer-in-residence happen, and Robin Perelle and the staff at *Xtra! West*, for publishing my column, "Loose End," for an unbelievable eight years now.

Once again, Brian Lam, Shyla Seller, Janice Beley, and the rest of the fine folks at Arsenal Pulp Press have to be acknowledged, not only for believing in me and my work, but for defying the odds and continuing to publish the kind of books that make me proud to work with a kick-ass independent Canadian publishing house.

I must also mention the many artists who have inspired me, either through our collaborations or just by being lucky enough to have been touched by their work. Veda Hille, Rae Spoon, Richard Van Camp, Dan Bushnell, Lyndell Montgomery, Anna Camilleri, Billeh Nickerson, Michael V. Smith, Elizabeth Hay, Cris Derksen, Kim Barlow, Kim Beggs, Elizabeth Bachinsky, Alison Bechdel, Charlie Chiarelli, and Dan Mangan, among others and in no particular order. I am proud and blessed to have crossed paths with all of you.